W9-BMP-244

The Ghost from Beneath the Sea

Also by Bill Brittain

ALL THE MONEY IN THE WORLD

WHO KNEW THERE'D BE GHOSTS?

THE FANTASTIC FRESHMAN

MY BUDDY, THE KING

WINGS

The "Coven Tree" Novels

DEVIL'S DONKEY

THE WISH GIVER

DR. DREDD'S WAGON OF WONDERS

PROFESSOR POPKIN'S PRODIGIOUS POLISH

BILL BRITTAIN

The Ghost from Beneath the Sea

drawings by Michele Chessare

HarperCollins*Publishers*

THE GHOST FROM BENEATH THE SEA

Printed in the United States of America.
For information address HarperCollins Children's Books,
a division of HarperCollins Publishers,
10 East 53rd Street, New York, NY 10022.

Library of Congress Cataloging-in-Publication Data
Brittain, Bill.
The ghost from beneath the sea / by Bill Brittain ;
drawings by Michele Chessare.
p. cm.
Summary: When a stranger comes to town and threatens to
turn the old Parnell mansion into an amusement park, three
spunky youngsters join forces with a trio of ghosts to outwit the plan.
ISBN 0-06-020827-9. — ISBN 0-06-020828-7 (lib. bdg.)
[1. Ghosts—Fiction.] I. Chessare, Michele, ill. II. Title.
PZ7.B78067Gh 1992 92-1091
[Fic]—dc20 CIP
AC

Typography by Elynn Cohen
3 4 5 6 7 8 9 10

For John Gawley—
Welcome to the family!

Contents

The Ghost from Beneath the Sea

A Really Strange Picture

Sure, a lot of people are scared of ghosts. But here in Bramton we really like 'em. We treat our ghosts just like neighbors.

In fact, they *are* our neighbors.

If that sounds kind of screwy, it's because you haven't heard the story I told a while back. It was about how Harry and Books and I stopped that scheming Avery Katkus from tearing down Parnell House and leaving Horace and Esmeralda with no roof over their heads and . . .

Horace and Esmeralda? Oh, they're our local ghosts.

Horace Parnell had his head cut off in 1777, at Saratoga in New York, while fighting for the colonies in the American Revolution. Esmeralda—we call her Essie—fell from the deck of a Mississippi riverboat and drowned in 1857.

Nowadays those two haunt Parnell House, which has been made into a fine museum. They don't show themselves much if strangers are about. That's a good thing, too, for they can be frightening sights if they appear unexpectedly. Horace often takes his head from its shoulders and carries it under his arm. Essie's silk dress, with its great hoopskirt, is always dripping wet, and she has water plants draped about her neck like green ropes.

Harry, Books, and I? We're real. I mean, we're not ghosts.

Harry's last name is Troy, but everybody calls him Harry the Blimp. He's really good-natured, and a lot of kids think he's just big and fat. But Harry's stronger than anybody else his age I know.

Get Books Scofield mad at you, and she's liable to feed you a knuckle sandwich. You'll be lucky to end up with nothing worse than a split lip. Books—her real name is Wendy—is smart, too. She reads a lot. That's why she's called Books.

I'm Tommy Donahue. According to my dad, I've got two left feet. I do everything wrong, from tripping over my untied shoelaces in church to drinking out of the finger bowl at our elementary school graduation banquet.

I guess that about takes care of all the introductions.

My tale this time really begins the day we three entered eighth grade, in September. Mrs. Cobb, our social-studies teacher, told the class we were each to write a l-o-n-g paper on "A Prominent Citizen of Bramton." It'd be due the second week in November.

Harry and Books were lucky. They got to write about Essie and Horace. A few evenings of interviews at Parnell House, and they'd be all set.

I was supposed to interview Asa Lubbock.

Asa Lubbock was a judge for thirty-five years before he retired a few months ago because of poor health. My dad, the village attorney, told me the judge was "tougher than shoe leather" and always stuck to the letter of the law. Once he even had his own son jailed for two days just for not paying a bill on time. I guess that's how Asa Lubbock got to be called "Old Lawbook."

When I called him on the phone, his voice was like a dog snarling. "Well? What do you want?"

I told him about my assignment.

"No interviews," he barked. "The law protects a man's privacy. I intend to keep it that way."

"But I just want to—"

"Good day, young man." He slammed down the receiver.

Since that phone call, I'd been afraid to contact him again. But Mrs. Cobb insisted that somehow I had to find a way to get my information. I was stuck.

But as it turned out, talking—or not talking—to Judge Lubbock was just a small problem. Like your hair being mussed up when you're floating in the middle of a shark-infested ocean.

The really *big* problem began on that Friday in mid-October.

Books and Harry decided to pay a visit to the Parnell ghosts to clear up a few details for their essays. I came along just for the fun of it.

We got to Parnell House at sundown. Because we'd helped save the place, the Bramton Village Council had voted to allow us to go inside whenever we liked, and we each had our own key. Harry used his to open the front door.

Books fumbled about in the darkness and finally found the light switch. Yeah, I know—there was no electric wiring back in 1748, when the house was built. But during the renovation, our mayor, Alonzo Peace, decided electricity was a lot more convenient—and less smelly—than candles or oil lamps. So he had it put in.

Anyhow, the big chandelier hanging from the ceiling and all the electrified candles lit up the place like noontime. Books closed the door, and we looked around.

No ghosts. Either they were somewhere else or they were staying invisible.

"Horace!" called Harry. "Essie! Come out, come out, wherever you are!"

Nothing.

We looked around for the circle of water that constantly formed under Essie's hoopskirt, even when you couldn't see her, and tried to sniff the stink of sweat and gunpowder that meant Horace was nearby.

Still nothing.

"They're probably upstairs," I said, "in the bedroom."

We headed for the stairs.

Suddenly Books stopped and pointed at the wall. "I don't remember ever seeing that before," she said.

There was a picture in a thick frame of gilded wood. The man in it seemed to be staring back at us. His face was all twisted up like he was hurting real bad, and his right hand was clutching at his chest.

He wore a dark suit, and the jacket had these small lapels. From the high, stiff collar of his shirt a necktie with a tiny knot hung down, with most of it covered by his vest. A chain was draped across the vest.

On the man's head was a derby hat.

"Somebody made a mistake, hanging that in here," said Books. "Those clothes aren't old-fashioned enough to belong to Horace's time—or Essie's, either. They're from the early 1900's."

"Where do you suppose that guy is standing?" asked Harry. "It's all dark, and I see stars in the sky behind him. And isn't that water?"

"And a ship of some kind?" I said. "His left hand seems to be grabbing a railing."

"Yeah, but ships float flat." Books made a back-and-forth motion with her hand. "This one is slanted, like the side of a mountain. Real screwy. What do you suppose . . ."

"Why don't we ask Horace and Essie about it?"

Harry suggested. "They ought to know."

"Good idea," said Books. "And I'm going to suggest to 'em that we get rid of the ugly thing."

We climbed the stairs. On the second floor we entered the main bedroom, where the two ghosts spent much of their time.

We'd no sooner closed the door than Horace and Essie appeared together. At first they were transparent, like drawings on glass. Then they became solid, standing by the window and peering out at the lights of Bramton.

"How nice of y'all to come callin'," said Essie as she turned about and made a damp little curtsy. "Come, Horace. Say hello to our guests."

Horace turned and bowed. At least his body did. His head remained on the table at the window, looking through the glass.

"Horace Parnell, you put your head back on its shoulders where it belongs!" commanded Essie in annoyance. "Land sakes, you have the manners of a street urchin. I don't know how I put up with your rude ways."

"But down on Spring Street, Chief Borchard is giving a ticket to a speeder," replied the head. "I want to see—"

"Do as I say, sir! This minute!"

Horace's hands took up the head and placed it on his shoulders. "Orders—always orders," he grumbled. "And from a mere girl, at that. In my time, Essie, children had respect for their elders."

"I'll not be called a child, Horace Parnell," replied Essie with an angry stamp of her foot. "I'm well over a hundred and fifty years old, and you know it."

Horace grinned and winked at us. He enjoyed teasing Essie whenever he got the opportunity.

"Now then," said Essie. "What can we do to amuse ourselves? A game of draughts, perhaps?" She glanced at an antique checkerboard on the desk by the far wall.

Both Horace and Essie liked playing "draughts," which is what they called checkers. But they could do it only when we came to visit and push the pieces around under their direction. Their own ghostly hands passed right through the "real" objects in the room.

"Before our game, a question, Young Thomas," said Horace. "'Tis about that newspaper you left when last you came."

"What about it?" I asked.

"On the uppermost page as it lay on the floor, I

glimpsed a picture of a man wearing trousers tucked in at the knee. He was shown swinging a mighty wooden club."

At first I didn't know what Horace was talking about. Then I got it. "That was a baseball player," I said.

"I know nothing of this . . . this baseball," Horace went on. "And I could see nothing of the story itself. But its title dismayed me: 'Yankees Wallop Indians.'"

"Horace, I—"

"D'ye think that be wise, Thomas—to attack the Indians with clubs? Long before our war for independence began at Concord Bridge, we Yankees had made peace with many of the tribes. So I do hope 'twas only the unfriendly Indians those Yankees walloped."

"It was just a game," I tried to explain. "Between two teams."

"Ah, I see. With colonists on the one side and Indians on t'other. Then they all take up clubs and begin beating at one another. I must say though, it does sound a bit dangerous for a mere game."

"But it's not dangerous. I mean, they weren't really Indians. I mean—"

"Some of our lads in disguise, I'll wager. The way 'twas done at the Boston Tea Party. Painting their faces and then sneaking out to those British ships . . ."

I looked at Harry the Blimp. He looked at me. Then we both began giggling. We just couldn't help it. Horace started to sulk.

It was Books who came to the rescue.

"Horace," she said, "please tell us about that picture downstairs. I don't remember seeing it here before. Where did it come from?"

"Picture?" Horace answered. "Which one? If you refer to the battle scene at Saratoga, it was painted by—"

"No, it isn't a painting. More like a photograph. But it's the ugliest thing I ever saw. A man on a tilted ship . . . at night. And the man has an awful expression on his face, like he's screaming in pain."

"Man? Tilted ship?" Horace thought this over and then shook his head so hard, I was afraid it was going to fall off. "I recall no such picture."

"Nor I," added Essie. "Let's go downstairs and you can show us the one you mean."

We left the bedroom, and Harry, Books, and I clumped back down the stairs. Horace and Essie kind of floated along beside us.

"Over there," said Books when we reached the ground floor. "Next to the window."

While the three of us waited, Essie and Horace glided across the room. They peered at the thing in the gilded frame, and Horace even removed his head and held it close to the glass.

"I don't know why anybody'd want that hanging in Parnell House," Books told them. "It's the most hideous thing I ever—"

"Hideous?" Essie repeated with a giggle. "You'll have to pardon me, but what I see in there is just gorgeous!"

"Gorgeous?" Harry the Blimp cried out in amazement. The three of us scurried across the room toward the ghosts. Then we all stared at the spot where we'd seen the picture.

The man and the ship and the nighttime scene were gone. What we now saw within the frame were Harry the Blimp and Books Scofield and Tommy Donahue, all staring back at us.

Our "picture" was just a mirror!

* * *

For the rest of the evening Horace and Essie kept teasing us about how we'd mistaken a mirror for a picture. I guess we had it coming, though, especially after the way Harry and I had laughed at Horace's interpretation of baseball.

But Harry and Books and I were still sure we'd seen a picture within that frame.

As we walked home later that evening, all we could talk about was the man on the tilted ship, clutching his chest and looking like he was about to scream.

"D'you think we just imagined it?" Harry asked. "Like the ghosts said?"

"No way," Books replied. "We couldn't all have imagined the same thing."

"Maybe the picture was in front of the mirror," I said. "And while we were upstairs, somebody sneaked in and . . ."

Books shook her head. "The picture was behind the glass. No, there's something really strange going on here."

"But what, Books?" I wanted to know.

None of us had an answer to that one.

As we passed by a streetlight, a couple of little kids darted by us. One of 'em was wrapped in a sheet, and the other looked like a pint-size Dracula. Halloween was still more than a week off, but I guessed they were getting in some early practice.

Finally we got to my house. "So long, you two," I said with a wave. "I'll see you tomor—"

Then I heard Dad call from the front porch. "Tommy? Books? Harry? Is that you?"

He was sitting there under the light with a book in his lap. Two more heavy, leather-bound volumes lay on the arm of his chair. Sometimes my father has to do a lot of reading just to keep up with his job.

"It's us, Dad," I called back. "We're not late, are we? I mean, it's not even nine—"

"Come up here on the porch. All three of you."

We all climbed the steps and gathered around Dad's chair. "What is it, Mr. Donahue?" asked Harry.

"About an hour ago," Dad answered, "I had a call from Mayor Peace—about Parnell House."

We all passed worried looks back and forth. If the mayor had called Dad late on a Friday evening to discuss something about the old house, there was trouble brewing for sure.

"About eighty years ago," Dad went on, "the last of the Parnells abandoned the old house. There was nobody to pay the taxes so the village took it over. That's why Alonzo Peace thought he had the right to fix it up and turn it into a museum."

"It's more than just a museum," said Books. "It's a home for Horace and Essie."

"And I hope it can stay that way," Dad replied. "But . . ."

"But what, Mr. Donahue?"

"There'll be a meeting in Alonzo's office first thing tomorrow morning. Since you three did so much to save the place, I thought you should be there."

"What's the meeting about?" Harry the Blimp asked.

"It . . . it seems Alonzo might have been mistaken."

"Mistaken? What do you mean?"

"A man came to see Mayor Peace today. And that man said he's the *real* owner of Parnell House!"

Summoning the Ghost

I didn't get much sleep that night. Books and Harry the Blimp and I—along with the ghosts—had already saved Parnell House once. If it was lost now, how would the new owner change the place? And what would happen to Horace and Essie?

We all arrived at Alonzo Peace's office in the Village Hall on the dot of nine the next morning. When we opened the door, the mayor was talking with another man.

He was big—even bigger than Harry the Blimp. Layers of flab made him bulge like a huge sack of potatoes. His face had red blotches on it, and little tufts of yellow hair sprouted from his head. His jacket was pink, and his tie was bright purple. His pants and shoes were white.

He reminded me of a great passenger balloon, full of hot air and getting ready to fly.

Mayor Peace got to his feet and made the introductions. The man's name was Hiram Flexx.

He stood up, stuck out a paw the size of a bath mat, and shook Dad's hand like he was pumping water from a well. "So you're the village attorney, Donahue," he roared as if we were two blocks away instead of right beside him. "Let's get this settled. I'd like to take possession of the Parnell estate right away."

Books, Harry, and I looked up at him with scowls on our faces. But Dad remained as cool as ice.

"Not quite so fast, please, Mr. Flexx. On the phone Alonzo said something about your having an official deed to the property."

Flexx yanked out a big piece of white paper from inside his jacket. "This is just a photocopy, of course," he said. "The original is tucked away in my lawyer's safe. It's two hundred fifty years old, so it's kind of fragile. But I think the copy will give you all

A. PEACE
DEED

the information you need."

Peering around Dad's arm, I could see that the paper had old-fashioned handwriting on both sides, with lots of fancy swirls and loops. Dad read it through carefully before turning to Mayor Peace. "This seems to be an old deed, which Abram Parnell had drawn up after he built the place."

"Well," rumbled the mayor, "since the deed's not registered with the village, we certainly don't have to—"

Dad shook his head. "If this deed is real, it was prepared well before Bramton ever existed. In those days whoever possessed the deed owned the land."

"Oh, the deed's real enough," Flexx told him. "Every transfer is recorded on the back of it."

Dad turned the paper over. "I see. First owner, Abram Parnell. He assigned it to his son Lorimer . . . then to Bradford Parnell . . . Letitia Parnell . . . Micah Parnell. . . . Aha."

"What is it, Ed?" asked the mayor.

"Parnells owned the house up until . . . uh . . . April 13, 1912. On that date an Ellsworth Parnell signed the deed over to an Addison Flexx."

"That was my great-grandfather," said Flexx. "He stuck it away in a trunk. That trunk was passed down in my family until I inherited it. I never figured the place was worth anything. But then I read a magazine article about how it'd all been fixed up, and—"

"You decided to just come and take over," said Mayor Peace angrily. "After we've spent nearly a million dollars repairing Parnell House and getting the antique furniture and—"

"I didn't ask you to do anything to my property," replied Flexx with a sly grin. "But since you've done it, I'll have a fine attraction for my amusement park."

"Amusement park!" gasped Books. "Right in the middle of town?"

"No law against it. And those three acres will be just about the right size. Of course I'll have to dig up that old graveyard and maybe move the house to some other—"

"No!" I cried out. "You can't move the house!"

"Yes I can, sonny boy. And I intend to do just that."

"Now just a second here," said Alonzo Peace. "There's still the matter of the back taxes. Since they weren't paid for over half a century, the village had every right to take possession."

Flexx shook his head. "My lawyer looked into the

matter. According to your own village laws, the legal owner must be notified of the taxes owed. I was never told of any taxes."

"Well I'm notifying you right now," bawled the mayor. "I'd imagine those taxes would come to . . . oh . . . at least a hundred thousand dollars."

Flexx yanked out a checkbook. "I'll pay this minute, if you like. A hundred thousand to get a property that's worth over a million? That sounds like a pretty good deal to me."

Dad waved a hand. "We can take care of that later. The real point here, Mr. Flexx, is that we never heard of any deed like this before you showed up. How do we know it isn't a fake?"

"Yeah, I thought we'd get around to that," Flexx answered. "Well, my great-grandfather Addison Flexx won that deed fair and square in a card game. I've got his old diary to prove it if that becomes necessary. As for the deed being real, somewhere in your village records you must have signatures of some of the people who signed it. Why not get an expert to compare them? That ought to be proof enough."

Dad and Mayor Peace and Books and Harry and I just stood there with our jaws flapping open.

"Well, I'll be getting along now," said Flexx with a toothy smile. "I think a week or ten days should be plenty of time for you to check out the deed. At the end of that time, I intend to claim my property. I'll be staying down at the Sheffield Inn if you need me for anything."

Before anybody could say another word, he was out the door and gone.

"Can . . . can he do it, Dad?" I asked fearfully. "Can Mr. Flexx take over the house just like that?"

"I have to say it doesn't look good," Dad answered. "Our only chance is to somehow prove that deed is a fake. But frankly I don't think there's much chance of that. Hiram Flexx seemed awfully sure of himself."

"I've got it!" Books cried out suddenly. "I've got it!"

Harry and I looked at her like she was nuts. "Got what, Books?" Harry said.

"No time for explanations," she said. She turned to my father.

"Mr. Donahue, how's chances of making me my own copy of that deed?"

"Well . . . sure, Books." Dad went to the copier in the corner of the office, put the deed on the screen, and pressed a couple of buttons. The machine began to hum. "But why do you want it?"

"I've got this idea. Trust me."

Books picked up the copy of the deed as soon as it slid out of the machine. Then she clutched Harry the Blimp's arm, and they headed for the office door. I looked at Dad and Mayor Peace, shrugged, and followed along.

* * *

"It's not fair. It's not fair! It's just not *fair*!"

That was me doing the grumbling as we followed Books in the direction of the Bramton Public Library. "After all we've done to save Parnell House for the ghosts and getting it all fixed up, Hiram Flexx walks right in and grabs it away."

Books wasn't very sympathetic. "Moaning isn't going to help, Tommy. We've got work to do."

I figured Books wanted to check out something about deeds and property. But what did she ask the librarian for?

"Mrs. Dawes, I need to find out how to summon a ghost."

Mrs. Dawes looked surprised. "We . . . we don't have much of a call for books on that subject," she said. "Let me look in the back. Maybe I can find something that will . . ."

She marched off toward the rear of the library.

"What do you need to summon ghosts for?" I asked. "We can go to Parnell House and see Horace and Essie any time we like."

"I don't want to see those two," Books replied. "I want to contact the *other* ghost."

"What other ghost?" Harry the Blimp demanded.

"The one on the ship—in the picture," said Books.

"That was just a mirror," said Harry. "We only imagined—"

"I don't think so," said Books. "I think we saw a picture of another ghost—a ghost that was trying to contact us. I'll bet anything it knows something about that deed of Flexx's."

"But why didn't the ghost come into the house and talk to us?" asked Harry. "Why did it just show up in a picture?"

"I think," said Books, "that it has to be invited inside. And the invitation has to be done in some kind of mysterious way. That's why I asked Mrs. Dawes for a book on . . ."

Just then the librarian returned. She carried a

book with a stained cover and yellowed pages.

"This is all I could find, Wendy," she said. "It was way up on a top shelf in the back. And I'm still not sure it'll tell you everything you want. . . ."

"If it's the only thing you've got," Books told her, "we'll have to work with it."

The title of the book was *The Occult.* It was so old that the pages cracked and split as they were turned.

"Here it is," said Books finally, pointing to the bottom of a page. "'Summoning ghosts.' We'll need a pentagram and—"

"A pentagram?" Harry asked. "Is that like a telegram? Are you going to send the ghost a telegram? Because if you are, I want to say—"

"A pentagram is a five-pointed star," I told Harry. "What else will we need, Books?"

"Some salt," she replied. "And candles. And . . . phooey!"

"What's wrong, Books?"

"The next page is missing. Torn out. I know the stuff we need to summon a ghost. But I don't know what to do with it."

"So what are we supposed to do now?" I asked.

"Tonight we meet at Parnell House," she said. "I'll have the things we need. We'll try everything we can think of. Somehow we'll get that ghost to appear."

"Sure," said Harry. "Something we do is bound to work."

I'd have agreed to anything that had the slightest chance of saving the house.

I just wish I was half as confident as Books and Harry seemed to be.

* * *

The full moon was hanging high in the sky as we approached Parnell House that night. Books was carrying a big paper bag.

"What's in there?" I asked.

"Chalk, a box of salt, and some old candles we had in our cellar," she said. "I made up a kind of chant, too. I hope that ghost will listen to it."

Essie and Horace were in the living room when we arrived. "Take seats, take seats, one and all," said Essie as soon as we'd entered. "Perhaps tonight we can beguile the time in pleasant conversation. Would you enjoy hearing of my trip down the Mississippi? Before I drowned, of course."

"Not that again," groaned Horace. "Have mercy, Esmeralda. You've told a thousand times how all those young men flocked about you. 'Tis enough to set my teeth on edge."

Essie stuck her tongue out at him. But before she could say anything further, Books spoke up.

"No time for chitchat tonight," she said. "There's work to be done. Let's get busy, 'cause I'm not really sure of how to do this and it might take a while."

"What are you trying to do?" Horace asked.

"Summon a ghost."

"But Essie and I—we're both right here. So why—"

"I mean *another* ghost. Harry, you and Tommy roll up the rug."

"What for?" Harry asked. "Do we need a rug to—"

"We need bare floor," said Books. "So I can draw the pentagram."

"You're going to scribble on our freshly waxed floors with chalk?" asked Essie, horrified. "Why, we could scrub until doomsday, and it might *never* come clean."

"And if I don't get busy and draw the pentagram," Books said, "you two ghosts might end up losing this whole house."

"Lose it?" rumbled Horace. "I thought Parnell House was ours forever. Books, what—"

"No time for explanations," Books snapped.

"But are we to be cast out of our home?" Essie

wailed, wringing her hands.

"Not if we can help it," said Harry the Blimp. He and I pulled away the rug and threw it into a corner. Books drew a large, five-pointed star on the planks of the floor.

"Now for the salt," she whispered.

"Salt?" exclaimed Essie. "You know best, of course, Books. But is it really necessary to—"

"Look, I'm doing the best I can!" Books replied peevishly.

Horace glared at Essie, who seemed to shrink under his gaze. "You . . . you do whatever you think proper, dear," she said in a quavery voice.

"Candles next." Books took five candles from her bag. She lit them and anchored them with their own wax at the points of the star.

"As a ghost," said Horace, "I have to tell you, Books, that arrangement wouldn't tempt me in the least to come calling. And those candles stink of rancid wax."

Books just glared at him. "Now for my chant," she said.

She took a slip of paper from her pocket. "After all my work, I just hope that ghost is listening right now."

She stepped among the candles and stood at the

center of the pentagram. "Okay," she began, and threw up her arms like a cheerleader.

"Gimme a G, gimme an H, gimme an O—S—T!
Parnell House is where you should be.
Go to the door and walk right through it.
Come on, ghost—you can do it!"

Silence. Books looked about as if she expected something to happen.

Nothing.

"What does that word 'gimme' mean?" Horace asked finally.

"I took a football cheer from school and changed it a little," said Books. "Don't give me a hard time, okay?"

"Here, ghostie, ghostie, ghostie," urged Harry as if he were calling a dog.

"It isn't working, Books," I told her.

"I should think not," said Essie. "My goodness, the star and the salt and candles and all this rigmarole would scare the stuffing out of any self-respecting ghost. What nonsense! If you ask me, it'd be better just to issue a polite invitation: 'Please drop in, ghost, and set a spell. We're ever so happy to meet you.'"

"Oh, come on!" Books protested. "We need magic here. D'you think any ghost would listen to—"

Suddenly every light in Parnell House—including the candles—went out.

There was a loud crack of thunder from outside, and a high wind sprang up. One of the shutters in an upstairs window came unfastened, and I could hear it banging against the siding.

Boom! . . . Boom! . . . Boom!—a loud pounding at the front door.

Harry the Blimp stumbled toward the door. He turned the knob.

Just as the door opened, the lights came back on and the candles flamed again.

Some . . . some *thing* was standing just outside.

At first it was misty and transparent, like a wisp of fog. Slowly it became more and more solid as it took the form of a human figure.

It was the man from the picture in the mirror!

His hand was still clutched to his chest. His face was a pasty white, and his mouth gaped open.

The man—the ghost—glided through the doorway and into Parnell House. As he did, the smell of cold sea air filled the room.

His lips curved into a smile. "At last," he said

with a deep sigh. “At last my journey is over.”

Harry the Blimp’s eyes were as wide and as round as soup bowls. “Who are you?” he sputtered.

The man swept his derby hat from his head and bowed low. “Parnell’s the name.”

Startled, Horace and Essie looked at the man and then at each other with gasps of astonishment. The new ghost spoke up again.

“Ellsworth Parnell, at your service!”

Ship of Doom

"Ellsworth Parnell!" exclaimed Books. "Boy, are we glad to see you. Now we can prove Hiram Flexx was lying. So tell us, Mr. Parnell—"

"Have patience, young lady," chided Essie. "Mr. Parnell, in addition to being our relative, is our guest. And I've no doubt he's had a long journey to get here. So give the man a moment, if you please, to catch his breath."

"Well . . . yeah, sure," Books replied. "Only—"

"Mr. Parnell, I am your ancestor, Esmeralda," said Essie, curtsying low. She introduced the rest of us. "And I'm ever so delighted to have you as a guest in our house."

"The man's no guest," rumbled Horace. "He's family. The house belongs to him as much as it does to us." He gave Ellsworth's hand a good shake. "Welcome home, sir."

"I was merely minding my manners," said Essie with a toss of her head. "And good manners are something about which you know nothing, Horace. So if you don't mind, the new Mr. Parnell and I would like to—"

"Shucks, ma'am. You can call me Ellsworth."

"Ellsworth—how delightful. Can I offer you some tea and biscuits?"

"We're ghosts, Essie," protested Horace. "We neither eat nor drink. So . . ."

By this time Books and Harry and I couldn't hold back our questions any longer.

"Why did you wait all this time to come back to Parnell House?"

"Was that really you in the picture in the mirror?"

"How did you die?"

"Did you really sign that deed?"

"Can you help us save this place?"

Ellsworth held up his hands. "Please, please!" he cried out. "I'll try to answer all your questions. But perhaps it would be best if I told everything in my own way."

"Fair enough," said Horace. He sat down on . . . nothing . . . and set his head comfortably in his lap. "Begin."

"Back in the early years of this century," said Ellsworth, "it was considered quite an adventure to tour the countries of Europe. I took such a tour early in 1912. By April, I was ready to return home. I booked passage on a brand-new luxury ship that would be sailing for the first time."

"Oh!" Essie cried out. "A boat trip. That's how I died, Ellsworth—from falling off a boat. Would you like to hear—"

"No!" we all shouted loudly.

"Go on with your story," Horace told Ellsworth. "If Essie gets to interrupting, we could be here forever."

"The ship was called the *Titanic*, and—"

"The *Titanic*!" Books exclaimed. "But that was the one—"

"You just hush up, Books," ordered Essie. "If I'm not allowed to interrupt, you aren't either."

"I could afford only a third-class cabin. Still, it

was most comfortable, with a deck where we could take the sun, and a gaming room. Alas, that gaming room. It was my downfall."

"Oh?" Horace put his head on its shoulders and leaned forward. "What happened?"

"It was there I met Addison Flexx."

Books and Harry and I gave each other worried looks. The Flexx family, it seemed, had been making trouble longer than we knew.

"While the *Titanic* visited ports in Europe and the British Isles, I struck up an acquaintance with Flexx, Charles Minton, and Lyle Arbuthnot. Shortly after we left Queenstown, Ireland, on April 11—that was a Thursday, as I remember—Flexx suggested we while away the time crossing the ocean by playing cards."

"Cards, huh?" Books didn't look at all happy. "For money?"

"Yes. Poker. At first Lady Luck distributed her favors evenly. But then Addison Flexx began winning almost all the larger pots. By Saturday evening I'd lost nearly all my own money. Then—late that night—came that final, disastrous hand."

"My daddy always said cards were the devil's playthings," moaned Essie.

"Your daddy has nothing to do with this story,"

snapped Horace impatiently. "Go on, Ellsworth."

"Both Arbuthnot and Minton had dropped out of play. My own hand, however, seemed unbeatable, and I saw a chance of regaining my losses. Each time Flexx raised the wager, I raised back. Finally, the last of my money was on the table. Again Flexx raised."

"You bet the deed to Parnell House, didn't you?" Books cried out accusingly.

Ellsworth nodded. "Youth and inexperience did me in. My hand was high. Addison Flexx's was higher. I . . . I lost everything. Including the family home."

"You didn't kill yourself over a card game, did you?" Horace asked in a grumble. "For that would be a coward's way, and I won't have a coward in my house, even if he is family."

"No," said Ellsworth with a shake of his head. "My loss was nothing compared with what occurred the following night."

"Oh my!" exclaimed Essie. "Tell us, Ellsworth."

"Sunday, April 14. We were steaming along at a brisk pace in spite of rumors of icebergs in the vicinity. And—"

"A moment, sir," said Horace. "What's an . . . an iceberg?"

"It's a hunk of ice floating in the ocean," answered Books impatiently. "Some of 'em are a lot bigger than . . . than this whole house."

"Nonsense! Ice and rime cannot grow to such a size."

"You must forgive Horace," Essie told Ellsworth. "He died in 1777, and he's still amazed by the motorcars he sees through the windows every night. Please continue."

"I was in my cabin, wondering how I'd be able to tell my brothers of the loss of Parnell House. Suddenly—shortly before midnight—I felt a slight bump and heard a scraping sound. Though I didn't know it at the time, the *Titanic* had rammed an iceberg. A hole was ripped in the ship's side. We were sinking."

"You drowned, then," said Essie. "What an awful fate. And so similar to my own. I must tell you, Ellsworth, about falling from the *Belle of Natchez* into—"

"Have done, Essie!" snapped Horace. "Why do you insist on prating like a squeaky door?"

"I didn't drown," Ellsworth continued. "When the ship began to tilt and I realized what was happening, I rushed up on deck. But all the lifeboats were either in the water or filled with people. I was in a panic. Suddenly I felt a great pain, like a huge ball of fire in my chest."

"Heart attack," Books whispered.

"Indeed, young lady. However, I managed to struggle back to my cabin, and I lay down on the bed there."

"Not too smart," said Harry the Blimp.

"True. But the pain and the fright had addled my brain. I lay there in agony as the boat sank lower and lower into the water. Then . . . the pain disappeared."

"You'd gotten well?" I asked.

"I died, lad. As a ghost I could look down upon my body there on the bed. And then the cabin filled with water. The lights went out."

"But why didn't you come back here to Parnell House?" asked Horace. "The way Essie and I did?"

"In the darkness I couldn't find the way. I was trapped! Years and decades passed."

"How awful for you!" Essie exclaimed.

"I kept dreaming of coming back here," said Ellsworth. "I tried in my thoughts to send a message home."

"The picture!" I blurted out. "The picture in the mirror!"

"Then—tonight—I got your invitation."

"Invitation?" I looked at Books.

"I knew it!" she cried out. "The pentagram and the salt and the candles—they worked after all."

"I know nothing of candles and such. What I heard was a gentle voice saying, 'Please drop in, ghost, and set a spell. We're ever so happy to meet you.'"

"What!" Books looked from Ellsworth to Essie and back again. "Do you mean I did all those things for nothing? And all Essie had to do was say—"

"Politeness is a virtue that transcends even magic," murmured Essie with a self-satisfied smile. "Go on, Ellsworth."

"Suddenly I was out of the ship and standing before the door of this house. You invited me inside. And you know the rest."

"A wond'rous tale indeed," said Horace. "We welcome you home, Ellsworth."

Essie turned to Harry and Books and me. "But you spoke of a threat to the house," she said. "I thought all our troubles were over back when the house was made into a museum."

"Something new has come up," Books told her. "You see, this guy Hiram Flexx has—"

"Flexx?" said Ellsworth. "Some relative of Addison Flexx, no doubt."

"Yes," said Books. "He says he owns this place. And he has the deed to prove it." She reached into her bag and held out the copy of the deed so that Ellsworth could read it. "But it's got to be a fake, right?"

"Unless . . ." Ellsworth began.

"Unless what?"

"Unless Addison Flexx managed to get to a lifeboat before the *Titanic* sank."

"Come on, Ellsworth," said Books. "This can't be real. I mean, okay, it's a photocopy, but—"

"Turn it over, please. Let me see the signatures."

Books flipped the deed to the back. Ellsworth peered at it.

"There," he said, pointing. "Even the place where the pen skipped as I was writing the date."

"You mean . . ." Books groaned.

"Alas, it's true," Ellsworth said. "The original of this document—all in proper form—is truly the deed to Parnell House, which Addison Flexx won from me on the *Titanic*."

* * *

"Good-bye, Parnell House," said Harry the Blimp glumly.

We didn't hang around long after that. We all

had to get up early for church the next day.

We walked along through the darkness, feeling sorry for ourselves—and for the ghosts of Parnell House.

At least I had a little good news when I got home. "Asa Lubbock called about an hour ago," Mom told me. "He's going to let you interview him after all. If you'll go to his house tomorrow right after church, he'll give you half an hour of his time."

"Jeez," I exclaimed. "I wonder what made him change his mind."

"I suspect Mrs. Cobb, your teacher, had something to do with it," Mom said, smiling. "She can be pretty persuasive—even with a crusty old judge."

"But just half an hour? That's not long enough to—"

"Take what you can get, Tommy."

Well, it was better than nothing. But only barely.

Dad was at work in his office. I shuffled in.

"You look like you've lost your best friend, Tommy," he said. "This business with Parnell House is really getting you down, isn't it?"

I nodded.

"Well, I think what Hiram Flexx wants to do is awful too. We really don't need an amusement park right in the middle of town. And after all the work you kids went to just to keep the house from being torn down . . . well, it's just a shame."

"And don't forget about the ghosts, Dad. There are three of 'em now."

I told him of the appearance of the new ghost and what Ellsworth had said about the deed.

"Those ghosts are as much a part of Bramton as anybody else," Dad replied. "They have a right to their own home. I wish I could think of something to help. But Flexx has got the law on his side."

"We can't just give up."

"I can delay Hiram Flexx for a few days. We'll even have the handwriting examined, though from what the new ghost said, it won't make much difference. In the end Flexx will own Parnell House. And he'll be able to do whatever he wants with it."

"Dad?"

"Yes, Tommy?"

"How would it be if you—and Mayor Peace maybe—met with the ghosts? You're a lawyer. Maybe you could think of something to—"

"Son, keeping Parnell House the way it is is as important to me as it is to you. Well, *almost* as important. But I don't want to get your hopes up just to have them crushed again. Besides, Alonzo Peace is terrified of the ghosts. So . . ."

I just stood there with my head bowed. I guess it made my father kind of nervous.

"Okay, okay," he said finally. "Alonzo and I will meet with the ghosts tomorrow. After everything you three kids have accomplished, I guess it's the least we can do. But don't expect too much."

He stared at the floor and shook his head mournfully.

"Don't expect anything, Tommy."

"At least we have to try. And . . . and thanks, Dad."

I left the office and went up the stairs to bed.

Sleep? Forget it.

A Game of Cards

Next day I felt kind of silly keeping my best suit on after church, with the necktie and the shiny black shoes, just to do a school assignment. But I guess Mom was right.

"If you're going to see Judge Asa Lubbock," she said, "you've got to look your best."

She drove me out to the little cottage where the judge lived at the edge of town. "I'll be back for you in thirty minutes," she said as I got out of the car and tucked my notebook under my arm.

"But Mom, it might take a little longer than . . ."

She smiled. "If Judge Lubbock said he'd give you half an hour, then that's what you'll get," she told me. "From all I've heard, he's a very precise man."

I walked up the steps and knocked at the door. It was opened by a woman in a white nurse's uniform.

"I'm Ms. O'Casey," she said after I'd told her my name. "I look after the judge. You're right on time, Tommy. He'll like that."

In the living room sat a man in a wheelchair. A shawl was wrapped about his thin, rounded shoulders, and he was wrinkled and seamed with age. His eyes glittered, he had a hawk's beak of a nose, and his thin lips neither smiled nor frowned but were like a single straight line slashed across his face.

"Sit down, Mr. Donahue." Judge Asa Lubbock's voice was harsh and stern. "What is it you want of me?"

I told him again about my assignment to interview him and write about his life.

"My life has already been written about in the official history of Bramton," he told me. "You could have read all about it down at the Village Hall without bothering me."

"Yes, sir," I said. "But maybe there are some

things you could tell me about yourself that aren't in that book."

"The law—that's all that interests me, young man."

"Oh . . . okay. Maybe we could talk about the law." I had to get something for my essay.

"Law is man's finest achievement," he snapped. "The Magna Carta in England . . . our own Constitution . . . right down to the rules and ordinances of our village of Bramton. The law gives mankind a pathway through the dense thicket of human relationships."

I was writing in my notebook as fast as I could. I wasn't quite sure I understood what the judge was saying, but I tried to get down every word.

"Trouble is, too many people try to bend the law to their own purposes. Take as simple a thing as illegal parking. According to our law, a ticket is written out and the driver appears in court. The fine is ten dollars, so that's what should be paid.

"But has our mayor, Alonzo Peace, or any of his Village Council ever paid such a fine? No indeed. First of all, no policeman would ever write a ticket on the mayor's car, wherever it was parked. And even if the ticket were written, most judges would not impose the fine. Yet is the mayor above the law? No indeed."

Wow! I'd once overheard Dad call Asa Lubbock "a tough old buzzard." Now I saw what he meant.

"They say," I began timidly, "that one time you put your own son in jail for forgetting to pay a bill. Is . . . is that true?"

"It is. And I'm proud to say that the sentence was carried out. My son had the money. He just forgot, in spite of repeated warnings. The penalty was written into the law. And after he'd spent two days in jail, he never forgot again."

I kept scribbling away in the notebook. Once Asa Lubbock got started, he didn't seem to need questions to keep him going.

"I became known far and wide for administering the law exactly as it was written, without fear or favor from any man," the judge continued. "Old Lawbook they called me, thinking it an insult. But I accepted the name proudly. Of all the decisions and rulings I ever made in my courtroom, I've never been ashamed of a single one."

"How long were you a judge, sir?" I asked.

"Near fifty years. I was on the state Supreme Court for some of that time. But what I miss most

are the days when I held trials down at the Bramton court. Ah, the people who would be brought in front of me. Having intentionally broken the law, they would then ask me to bend it for them. 'Have mercy on me,' they'd plead. But I gave them justice instead."

Boy, I thought, I'd sure hate to be judged by Asa Lubbock.

"In time," said the judge, "I was charged with being too stern in my judgments. 'You're getting old,' people said. 'You should have a rest.' And so they forced me to retire. But it took them three years to do it, as I insisted that the law be followed at every step. Now I have only a little time left on this earth. But I find myself wishing for just one more case."

"One more case, sir?"

"Indeed." The judge stared off into the distance, and his expression became even more stern. "One case—perhaps something with an unusual twist to it. One last case by which I could again show that the law is a guiding beacon for all men. To sit on that bench down in the village and be once more a judge rather than a cripple in a wheelchair. One final day in court for Old Lawbook!"

At that, Judge Lubbock bowed his head and drew

the shawl closer about his shoulders. “Now,” he mumbled gruffly, “I suspect our time is up. Go, Thomas Donahue. Go and write your school essay about what a harsh old man you found Asa Lubbock to be. I ask only that you write honestly about what I have told you.”

A man as tough as shoe leather and as hard as flint, I thought while waiting at the curb for Mom to pick me up.

So why did I find myself feeling sorry for him?

* * *

Dad kept his promise. Somehow he talked Alonzo Peace into meeting with the ghosts on Tuesday night.

We picked Alonzo up at about eight thirty. He sat up front with Dad, while Books and Harry the Blimp and I were crammed into the rear seat. “Are . . . are you sure it’s safe?” the mayor asked before he’d even closed the door. “I’ve read some awful things about ghosts.”

“Don’t be scared, Mayor Peace,” said Books. “Remember that night last year when we found the Parnell Parchment? You saw Horace and Essie then. What’s there to be afraid of?”

“A lot,” the mayor told her. “I could look right

through both of them, and Horace kept taking his head off, and the girl kept dripping water onto the floor. Now you tell me there's a third ghost. I don't like this. I don't like it at all."

"But the ghosts are real nice," said Books.

"I'll risk one visit," said the mayor. "But the first time anything strange starts happening, I'm leaving!"

Strange? With ghosts? I wondered if we'd have to tie Mayor Peace down just so he wouldn't run away on us.

The ghosts did their best not to scare Dad or the mayor. They were waiting for us in the living room of Parnell House when we opened the door, and they looked solid, not transparent, the way they sometimes appeared. Horace even had his head placed on his shoulders instead of tucked under one arm.

Of course, there wasn't anything that could be done about Essie's dripping hair and clothing, and Ellsworth did look kind of ghastly, with his pale face and bluish lips. But somehow we got the mayor steered to the biggest chair, where he sat wide-eyed and trembling.

"I have to tell you, things don't look good for the

future of Parnell House," Dad said to the ghosts after all the introductions had been made. "We had hoped to prove Hiram Flexx's deed was a fake, but Ellsworth's identification of it put an end to that idea."

"I sorely regret my words," said Ellsworth with a shake of his head. "Yet I had to be honest."

"It really doesn't make much difference," Dad told him. "If you hadn't identified the deed, there were a lot of other ways he could prove it was real. I guess Flexx has us right where he wants us."

"It's not fair!" Horace rumbled. "After everybody in Bramton expended so much effort and all that money to restore this house, Flexx comes along and just takes it. I say we pinion the scoundrel in the pillory or stocks until he agrees to do right by us."

"The pillory and stocks aren't used for punishment anymore," said Dad. "No, our only chance is to somehow prove the deed itself isn't legal. If we could show that Flexx stole it, for example, there'd be no problem. But with Ellsworth's signature right there on the back, there's no question that he wanted Flexx's great-grandfather to have it."

"It's not what I wanted at all," said Ellsworth. "But Addison Flexx won the deed in the game. As a man of honor, I had to turn it over to him."

"Poker!" snorted Essie. "If you ask me, that game is pure evil. When I was riding that riverboat down the Mississippi, there were ever so many fine young gentlemen I longed to keep company with. But the only thing on their minds was sitting in the public room with a handful of cards. Poker, poker, poker—ugh!"

Suddenly Mayor Peace stopped shaking and leaned forward in his chair. "Poker?" he exclaimed. "Did somebody mention poker?"

"Yes, Alonzo," said Dad. "Are you familiar with the game?"

"Why, I'm the craftiest, the cleverest, and—yes—the smartest poker player that ever . . ." Suddenly, with a glance at Books and Harry and me, the mayor fell silent. Then he cleared his throat loudly.

"Ahem . . . er . . . uh . . . That is to say, I do play an occasional hand. Purely for amusement, of course. No money on the table. As we all know, gambling isn't allowed in this state. We use matchsticks just to keep score."

Alonzo pulled out a big handkerchief and mopped his brow. "It might be best," he went on, "if we didn't mention anything about poker to my wife,

Cora. She doesn't approve of it."

"Of course not, Alonzo," said Dad. "But you are familiar with the game?"

"Somewhat," Mayor Peace replied. "Ellsworth, why don't you tell us about these poker games you had on the *Titanic*."

"Alonzo," said Dad, "I really don't think we have to embarrass Ellsworth by—"

"Hush up, Ed," ordered the mayor. "I have a reason for asking. Go on, Ellsworth."

"There were four of us," said the ghost. "Addison and I had been joined at our table in the gaming room by Lyle Arbuthnot and Charles Minton. It was Flexx who suggested we play a few hands of poker.

"At first, Lyle and Charles wanted to back out, pleading that they knew little of the game. But Addison and I, being the more skilled, explained the rules and the desirability of having at least four players. Lyle and Charles reluctantly agreed to sit in. A ship's steward fetched us a couple of decks of cards. I opened one deck, removed the jokers, and—"

"Hang on a minute," said the mayor. "Are you sure the cards came from the steward?"

"Yes," Ellsworth replied. "Each deck was blue,

with the *Titanic* symbol on the backs. They were quite handsome."

"What were you thinking of, Alonzo?" asked Dad.

"I was wondering if Addison Flexx had brought in a deck of marked cards—the kind you can read from the back," said the mayor. "But if they were from the ship, that couldn't be the case. Unless, of course, Flexx had taken them back to his cabin one night and marked them in some way."

Ellsworth shook his head. "Whenever we weren't playing, I kept the cards," he said. "Addison Flexx insisted on this."

"Well, so much for that idea," said Mayor Peace. "It appears to me the game was honest enough as far as the cards were concerned."

I guess Mayor Peace had about gotten over his fear of the ghosts. The talk of poker was just too interesting.

"We always sat in the same chairs," said Ellsworth. "Lyle Arbuthnot was at Addison Flexx's left. Then Charles Minton. And finally, me. As the deal moved around the table, the next dealer would shuffle one deck while the other was in play.

"As I recall," he continued with a chuckle, "Lyle

Arbuthnot, in his innocence of the game, had problems with its etiquette. He would, for example, ask to see the hands of others once he'd dropped out of play. Or he'd become angry and throw down his cards if he lost too many pots. Addison chided him about this more than once.

"At any rate, a pattern of play soon developed. Lyle, Charles, and I would win hands in which only small bets had been made. But whenever there was a lot of money on the table, Addison Flexx always seemed to have the best cards. This went on for three days."

"What do you think, Alonzo?" Dad asked. "Was there any cheating?"

"Maybe," said the mayor. "Or maybe Addison Flexx was just a smarter player than the others. I sure haven't heard any real proof of cheating so far. But say, Ellsworth, let's get to that final hand—the one where you lost the deed."

"The game was draw poker—nothing wild," said Ellsworth.

"Who was dealing?" Alonzo asked.

"Charles Minton."

"Oh, nuts!" exclaimed the mayor. "If it'd been Flexx, I'd be certain there was some hanky-panky."

"Can we hold on here a minute?" said Books suddenly. "I don't know much about this poker. From the looks on their faces, Tommy and Harry don't either. So could you kind of explain it as you go along. I mean, what's this 'draw' poker? And 'nothing wild'?"

"In the game as we were playing it," said Ellsworth with a smile, "the players are dealt five cards apiece. Each player may exchange one, two, or three cards from his hand for the same number of new ones. The object is to improve what you have in your hand."

"I see," said Books. "At least I think I do."

"Wild cards," Alonzo interrupted, "can be used in place of any other card the player needs. If twos are wild, for example, a two could be used as an ace or a king or anything else."

"But in this case," added Ellsworth, "nothing was wild."

"Okay," said Books with a shake of her head. "Go on, Ellsworth."

"After we'd all drawn our new cards," said Ellsworth, "the betting began. Charles Minton dropped out at once. He had nothing. There was a round of raises and—"

"Here we go again," said Books. "What's a raise?"

"It's when somebody increases the bet," said Alonzo. "The other players have to match it or else stop playing."

"And stop is just what Lyle Arbuthnot did," said Ellsworth. "That's when he committed another fault against the customs of the game."

"What did he do?" I asked.

"After dropping out of play, he showed his hand. Addison Flexx became furious. 'Never expose your cards unnecessarily!' he roared. 'No player should *ever* do so, even when the hand is ended!'

"I thought Addison's criticism was somewhat extreme. After all, Lyle was just a beginner. And his three of a kind certainly didn't threaten my—"

"Three of a kind?" Books was determined to understand what was going on.

"Three cards of the same number," the mayor told her. "Like three eights, or three aces."

"Is that . . . that three of a kind a pretty good hand, Mayor Peace?"

"Quite good, in a game such as this."

"But Lyle Arbuthnot quit with 'em, huh?"

"Lucky for him," said Ellsworth. "You see, I was holding a jack-high straight fl—"

"If you keep using all those funny words, we're going to be here all night," Books said. "What exactly did you have, Ellsworth?"

"My pardon, Books. My cards were all in the hearts suit. I held the seven, eight, nine, ten, and jack."

"Holy St. Peter's sandals!" exclaimed Alonzo.

"Pretty good, huh?" Books asked him.

"In draw poker—with nothing wild—I'd bet everything I own on such a hand," said the mayor with a shake of his head.

"That's just what I did, Mayor Peace," said Ellsworth mournfully, "including the deed to this house. Addison Flexx matched my bet. 'I'll see what your hand is,' he demanded. So I showed my cards. Then Addison showed his."

"And they were . . ."

"Ten, jack, queen, king, ace—all in spades."

"A royal flush!" Alonzo Peace flopped back into his chair. "Unbeatable!"

By this time, Books had pulled a notebook out of the pocket of her jeans and was writing in it with a pencil. "Lemme get this straight," she said. "First Minton quits. After that, Mr. Arbuthnot gets out, even though he has three cards of the same kind. Ellsworth, you have the seven up to jack of hearts.

But you get beat because Mr. Flexx has ten through ace—all spades."

"That's it exactly," said Ellsworth.

"Okay, Mr. Mayor. Your turn. You're the poker expert. Was the game all honest?"

"The hands held by Ellsworth and Mr. Flexx were both very high for such a game," said Alonzo. "But if there was any cheating, I don't know how it was done."

"Marvelous—just dandy," moaned Books, scowling. "So what do we do next, Mr. Donahue?"

"There's not much left *to* do, Books," said Dad. "I've tried to delay things as much as possible for the sake of you three—and the ghosts. But I can't hold off any longer. Tomorrow I'll call Hiram Flexx and tell him he's the new owner of Parnell House."

"Dad?"

"Yes, Tommy?"

"Could you wait until after school to tell him?"

"Sure, I guess so. But why?"

"Books and Harry and I saved this place once for the ghosts. I think we should be there when we finally lose it."

Hiram Flexx Meets the Ghosts

On my way to school the next morning, I passed a couple of parked cars that had WASH ME scrawled across their windshields with soap. Halloween was only a couple of days away, and I guess some of the kids in town were getting in a little practice with their pranks. No real harm done. A little soap and water, and the glass would be as good as new—and probably a whole lot cleaner.

I remembered what fun it was getting dressed up in a costume and painting my face with green and red and going around to the neighborhood houses with a big bag for trick or treat. But now I was too old for such stuff.

Sometimes growing up can be a real drag.

In social-studies class Mrs. Cobb reminded us again that we all ought to be hard at work on our essays about Bramton's notable people. They had to be at least ten pages long. The things Judge Asa Lubbock had told me were real interesting, but I still didn't have enough material for more than about three pages.

After school Dad picked up Harry the Blimp and Books and me. "I guess once this meeting's over Hiram Flexx will own Parnell House, huh, Dad?" I asked.

"Well, not quite that fast," he told me. "A new deed has to be made out and registered with the village. Flexx still has to pay the back taxes and—"

"Back taxes!" snorted Books. "Big deal. The house and property are worth ten times what he'll pay in taxes. Flexx comes in and takes over just like that. I get so mad, I could—"

"It's no use getting angry," Dad said. "Fixing the place up was a big mistake, no doubt about it. But how were we to know somebody else owned it?"

"I'm really worried about Horace and Essie—and

Ellsworth, too," I said. "What'll happen to them after—"

"Maybe Hiram Flexx will change his mind," Harry the Blimp put in. "Maybe he'll keep the house and let the ghosts stay."

"Sure he will," Books snorted. "But only if he can figure out some way to charge 'em rent. And how are the ghosts going to get any rest during the day with an amusement park going full blast all around 'em?"

Still grumbling, we reached the Village Hall and went up to Mayor Peace's office. The mayor and Hiram Flexx were waiting for us.

Once we'd all gotten seated, Mayor Peace leaned forward in his chair. "Mr. Flexx," he began, "our investigation indicates that you do indeed have some claim on Parnell House."

"I have a lot more than 'some claim,' Peace," said Flexx in a voice that could be heard in the next county. "I own the whole place, lock, stock, and barrel. It's mine to do whatever I want with."

"And do you still intend to put in an amusement park?" Dad asked.

"Sure. I can make a lot of money that way."

"But Bramton is a small town," Dad went on.

"Have you given any thought to how much such a noisy place would disturb our peaceful village?"

"What do I care? I won't be living nearby. I'll hire people to run the park and collect all the money. A lot of tourists come to see Parnell House. When I'm done, they'll be paying to ride a roller coaster and eat a hot dog as well."

A roller coaster and hot dogs at Parnell House. To me it sounded as bad as putting a merry-go-round in front of the Statue of Liberty.

"There's no law against it, is there?" Flexx asked the mayor.

"No," replied Alonzo with a sad shake of his head. "But I was hoping, Mr. Flexx, that you'd be more reasonable."

"Hey. I'm a reasonable man. Are you talking some kind of a deal, Mayor? So you can get back the Parnell property?"

Dad and Alonzo looked at each other hopefully. Maybe there was still a chance to . . .

"How much, Mr. Flexx?" asked the mayor. "How much would you want to sell the property back to the village of Bramton?"

Hiram Flexx leaned back in his chair with a toothy grin. "Two million dollars."

"Two million!" exclaimed Mayor Peace. "Impossible! Why, if we doubled the taxes of everybody in town, we couldn't come up with that amount in ten years."

"Then I guess this meeting is over," said Flexx, getting to his feet. "I'll expect you to turn Parnell House and the property over to me within ten days. I want to get work done on the park before winter comes. Now, I guess I'll go over and take a look at the place."

With that, Flexx walked out, leaving the rest of us sitting in miserable silence.

* * *

"Lemme see. If the Ferris wheel goes there, then the cotton-candy booth can stand just beside it and . . ."

Hiram Flexx was strolling about the Parnell grounds and talking loudly to himself. He had a notebook in his hand, and every now and then he'd write something in it.

Harry the Blimp and Books and I were crouched down behind tombstones in the little graveyard in back of the house. After leaving the mayor's office, we'd followed Flexx. Don't ask me why. I guess we all had a crazy idea that we could still come up with some plan to save the house—and the ghosts.

"Then the baseball throw and the water slide," Flexx went on. "And maybe . . ." Suddenly he stopped and stared at his notebook.

"Why, I forgot all about the shooting gallery," he said. "Great Caesar's ghost! What a stupid mistake."

I felt Books's elbow jab hard against my ribs. "Tommy," she whispered. "Harry. That's it!"

"What's it, Books?" I whispered back.

"Ghost. I mean ghosts."

"What are you getting at, Books?" asked Harry. "Once Flexx takes over, the ghosts are done for."

"Maybe." Books chuckled. "But I don't think Hiram Flexx believes in the ghosts of Parnell House."

"He'll meet 'em soon enough, after he owns the place," I said.

"Maybe he should meet those three real soon, Tommy. Like tonight."

"But why?"

"Think back," Books told me. "I know when I first looked at Horace and Essie, I almost screamed."

I began to see what Books was getting at. "So maybe the Parnell ghosts could scare Flexx so much he wouldn't want the place after all—is that it?"

"Right. Come on, Tommy. You too, Harry. Let's go have a little talk with Mr. Flexx."

We got up from behind the tombstones and walked toward where Flexx was making notes in his little book. "Hi there, Mr. Flexx," said Books in a real friendly voice.

He turned and stared at us. "What do you kids want?" he asked. "I don't like you hanging around on my property."

"It's not yours quite yet," I said. "There's still a lot of paperwork, and the back taxes to be paid."

"But we thought you might like a little tour of the house," said Harry. "Seeing as how you'll soon own it."

"I've already seen the house. Last week. I paid my admission and the guide took me all through it."

"Oh, but that was during the daytime," Books said. "You can't really get the full . . . uh . . . beauty of the place until you've seen it at night."

"Yeah, the gho—" Suddenly Books kicked me in the ankle—hard! She glared at me, but when she turned back to Flexx, she was smiling again.

"What Tommy's trying to say," she went on sweetly, "is that when the lights are on and it's dark outside, the house looks really different. You should see it then, Mr. Flexx. You really should."

"But the place is locked tight after six."

"Oh, we have keys," Harry the Blimp told him. "We'd be glad to let you in."

"Hmm," muttered Flexx. "Y'know, maybe you're right. Perhaps I should have a look at night. If it's as good as you say, I can raise my admission price to it once the sun goes down."

"Why don't you meet us here later?" said Books. "When it's real dark."

"That's very sweet of you, little girl," Flexx told her. At that "little girl" crack, I saw Books clench her fists. But she kept a big smile plastered on her face.

"Suppose I meet you all here at about eight thirty?" Flexx went on.

"Nine o'clock would be better. We've got to make pla—"

This time I got to kick Books in the ankle. "We have to finish our homework first," I said.

"Okay, nine o'clock. And since you're doing this favor for me, I'll give you all free tickets for a ride on my roller coaster—just as soon as it's built."

* * *

"Now the three of you have got to be spookier than you ever were in your lives."

The hands of the clock on the wall of Parnell House pointed to twenty minutes before nine.

Books and Harry and I were preparing the ghosts for Hiram Flexx's visit.

"I think we should start with your head, Horace," Books went on. "If you could somehow make it appear right in front of Flexx's face . . . and then give out with some moans and groans . . ."

"You just leave everything to us," said Essie. "We'll frighten the very liver out of that wicked man."

"Okay. But you'll have to be really good at it. This is the last chance we've got."

"I . . . I'm not at all sure of what this is all about," said Ellsworth. "Are some humans really that afraid of mere ghosts?"

"They are indeed," Horace told him. "The first time I appeared to Tommy here, he shook as if with the ague. D'you recall that, Young Thomas?"

"I sure do. If the three of you are that good with Hiram Flexx, he won't stop running until he reaches Canada."

"Now here's how it'll work," said Books. "We'll get Flexx inside. Once he's in, I'll go to the light switch. Harry, you have your key ready. Then one—I turn off the lights so he's left in the dark. Two—Harry and Tommy and I run outside, leaving Flexx here alone. Three—Harry locks the door so Flexx can't leave."

She turned to the ghosts. "After that, it's up to you three."

"We'll perform our roles properly, never fear," said Essie. "Once—before my death—I took a part in an amateur play. *The Villain of Venice,* it was called. And I was superb, if I do say so myself. Everyone who saw it said I was the most—"

"Modesty was never one of your faults, Esmeralda," said Horace. "I wonder if, just this once, we could dispense with your inordinate bragging. The time grows short, and Mr. Flexx could be here at any moment."

Essie poked out her lower lip. "Oh, pooh, you ol' killjoy. I wasn't bragging but simply telling the truth. Yet perhaps you're right. Maybe the three of us should, for the moment, just fade away."

With that, the three ghosts became first transparent—then invisible.

Books, Harry the Blimp, and I went outside into the night.

Not long afterward a car came to a stop in front of the old house. Hiram Flexx got out. "Are you three kids around somewhere?" he called.

"Over here, Mr. Flexx," I answered.

Flexx plodded to where we were standing. "Well, let's see what my house looks like after dark," he said. "Lead the way, kids."

We went inside. Flexx looked around. "Hey, you weren't kidding," he told us. "The place is a lot different after dark. It reminds me of that big scene in *Gone With the Wind* where . . ."

Books sidled off toward the light switch. At the same time Harry the Blimp reached into his pocket for his key. I moved to where I wouldn't miss the doorway, even in the dark.

Flexx walked to the far side of the living room and took a chair. He was looking right at Books, so she pulled her hand away from the switch. I wondered how long he was going to sit there.

"Hey, look at that candlestick," he said suddenly. "I'll bet it's solid silver. It must be worth a lot of money."

He got up and began walking across the room.

Snap! The room was completely dark.

"Hey!" called Flexx. "What's going . . ."

I lunged toward the doorway. Just as I got there, I ran into Books. We stumbled outside, where Harry the Blimp was already waiting. He slammed the door behind us.

Click! I heard Harry's key turn in the lock.

"Got him!" whispered Books with a chuckle.

All three of us moved to one of the front windows. We wanted to see the ghosts in action.

The living room was still dark. We could hear Hiram Flexx stumbling around and muttering to himself. "Are you kids still in here? Where's the . . ."

Then he found the switch and turned the lights back on. "Where in blazes did everybody go?" he cried out.

He tried the door. It rattled but didn't open.

With a shrug he turned around. He walked back to where the silver candlestick sat on its table. Then he leaned over to look at it more closely.

Slowly Horace Parnell's head came into view *between* Flexx's eyes and the candlestick. We could see Flexx blink as the head grew more and more solid. The noses of man and ghost were only inches apart.

Horace's mouth opened. He began an eerie moaning.

"Perfect!" crowed Books beside me. "Just perfect!"

"What . . . what's *this*?" we heard Flexx say in little more than a whisper.

"It's just a li'l ol' head, Mr. Flexx."

Flexx spun about. Just behind him stood Essie—

or at least some of her. She'd decided to remain transparent. River plants were twined about her, and water dripped from her wide skirt onto the floor.

"They're doing a great job," said Harry the Blimp. "Ol' Flexx must be scared out of his mind!"

The rest of Horace's body appeared in a corner of the room. The hands reached out, took up his head, which was still moaning, and put it onto his shoulders.

Flexx staggered to a chair and flopped down into it.

Essie kind of floated through the air until she was hovering just above where Flexx sat. Then she arranged herself so that she appeared to be sitting on his lap.

Ellsworth Parnell, with his ghastly white face and bluish lips, popped into view by the fireplace. He lifted his arms menacingly.

"Hiram Flexx!" he howled in a quavering voice. "I've come for you!"

Not such a great performance, really, I thought. But after all, he'd spent most of his . . . his ghost-hood . . . down at the bottom of the ocean, so he didn't have much experience at scaring people. I know if I'd been the one inside, seeing those ghosts for the first time, I'd have been frightened out of my mind.

Essie drifted away from Flexx's lap, leaving a damp spot on his pants from her soggy skirt. He leaned forward, placing his face in his cupped hands. Then his body began heaving and shaking.

"We got him!" Books yipped. "We did it. He's so scared he's . . . he's . . ."

Then the sound came to us through the window. It was the last one we'd ever expected to hear. When Flexx raised his head, his mouth was wide open, and the noises he made were—

"He's laughing!" Harry the Blimp cried in outrage. "He isn't scared at all."

It was true. Flexx looked from one ghost to another. As he did, the sounds got louder and louder.

"Ha, ha, ha! Oh, ho! This is a good one! What a thing to happen. Ha, ha, ha. Ho, ho! Ghosts—three of 'em! Who'd have thought I'd be so lucky. Ha, ha, ha!"

"D'you suppose he's lost his mind?" asked Harry.

"Naw," Books replied. "I think he's just happy. Jeez, who'd have thought it?"

"Come on in here, you kids," Flexx called. "I

know you're hiding around here someplace. And you ghosts, you stay right where you are. Oh, this is rich. This is really marvelous! Oh, ho, ho. Ha, ha!"

Well, we couldn't keep Hiram Flexx a prisoner in Parnell House forever. We went to the door. Harry put his key in the lock and twisted.

As we opened the door, Hiram Flexx's laughter told us we'd failed—for probably the last time—to save Parnell House.

"Ho, ho, ho! Ha, ha, ha!"

One Magic Night a Year

"Oh, this is good!" Flexx hooted. "This is really something! I'll bet you kids thought that when I saw these three ghosts, I'd go running off into the night with my tail between my legs. But let me tell you, it takes more than a few ghosts to scare Hiram Flexx."

Books and Harry the Blimp and I looked at the ghosts and shook our heads sadly. We'd failed again.

"Oh, I'll admit to being a bit startled when the head and the wet gal and the guy in the derby first appeared," Flexx went on. "But as soon as I saw they couldn't do anything but make funny noises, I knew I didn't have anything to worry about."

"I will not be referred to as a 'gal,' Mr. Flexx," said Essie with an angry stomp of her foot. "Nor is Ellsworth Parnell a 'guy.' This is our home, and I must insist that you treat us with respect."

"Your home?" Flexx started laughing again. "Not for much longer. In a few days, I'll own the whole shebang."

"Then let me warn you," said Horace. "Esmeralda, Ellsworth, and I have made up our minds. As long as the walls of Parnell House still stand, we will inhabit it. There's no way you can drive us out."

"Drive you out?" said Flexx. "Are you kidding? I want you here."

I couldn't believe my ears. Hey, maybe Hiram Flexx wasn't as bad as I'd thought. But then he went on.

"What an attraction you three will make. The amusement park will be taking in money for me all day long. Then, after dark, I open up this place. People will be standing in line to buy tickets and see the ghosts. Day or night, there'll always be something to bring in the customers."

"D'you mean you're gonna turn Horace and

Essie and Ellsworth into a . . . a *sideshow?*" I gasped.

"Sure. Why not? The three of 'em can work up a little act, with some singing and dancing and maybe a few jokes thrown in, and—"

"I'd never be a party to anything so degrading," said Essie with a toss of her head. "And neither, I'm sure, would Horace or Ellsworth."

Both of the other ghosts nodded in agreement.

"Come on," Flexx pleaded. "Be reasonable. I'll pay you whatever—"

"We have no need for money," said Horace grimly.

"Isn't it enough that your amusement park will constantly be disturbing our rest during the daylight hours?" added Ellsworth. "Do you also expect us to make fools of ourselves at night? I say no to you, sir. A thousand times no!"

"You can't talk to me that way," replied Flexx angrily. "I own this house. And the way I see it, you ghosts are part of the bargain."

"We're not part of any bargain you've made," said Horace firmly. "I remind you, Mr. Flexx, that we ghosts were never involved in the dealings you had with the officials of Bramton."

"Okay then," replied Flexx with a sneer. "If that's

how you're going to be, then as soon as I take over this house, I'll hire somebody who knows a way to get rid of ghosts. And out you go—all three of you!"

"You . . . you wouldn't dare try such a thing," gasped Essie.

"Just wait, little lady."

"It's just not right!" Horace exploded. "The U.S. Constitution says that people are protected in their homes from unreasonable search and seizure."

At that, Flexx chuckled loudly. "You're not people," he said. "You're ghosts."

"We certainly are people!" Essie exclaimed. "Just because we can disappear when we want to, and even though Horace has a head he can put on and take off like a hat, doesn't mean—"

"Come on, girlie. The Constitution wasn't written for ghosts. Face it—I've got the law on my side."

When I heard Flexx say that, an idea popped into my head. Would it work? I didn't know. We sure hadn't been very successful up to now.

But I had to try.

"Interesting, isn't it?" I said, like I was talking to Books and Harry. "Are ghosts people? What a case this would make in a court of law."

"Court of law?" said Flexx. "Don't be ridiculous."

"Are ghosts people?" I repeated. "If they're not—if you're right, Mr. Flexx—then they'd just be part of the house, like the chairs and tables. And they'd have to do whatever you told them. They'd really add a lot to your amusement park."

Books caught on to my plan right away. "People would be standing in line to see 'em," she added. "You'd be rich, Mr. Flexx."

"Yeah." Flexx rubbed his hands together greedily. "Yeah."

"Of course, there's always the outside chance the law would say they are people," I told him. "And that would complicate things for you. A trial would be a gamble. And I guess you're not the gambler your great-grandfather was."

Flexx stared at me for a long time. "Compared to me," he said finally, "Great-grandpa Addison was a piker. I'm a real gambler. Whether it's the turn of a card or the way the dice fall, I—"

"Would you dare to gamble on a trial, then?" I asked him.

"Well . . . maybe. If the reward for winning were high enough."

"A real haunted house in your amusement park," I said. "Real ghosts for your customers to look at.

There's never been such a thing before."

"Money," said Books. "Lots of money."

Flexx thought about this. Then he snapped his fingers and nodded. "Okay, a trial then—to show that ghosts aren't real people. But what court would hear such a case?"

I hadn't thought about that. For a moment I was speechless.

Then an idea popped into my head.

"I can think of a judge—" I began.

"I get it. Pretty tricky. You get some local guy who doesn't like my taking over Parnell House. He'd be so prejudiced, I'd never get a fair hearing."

"The judge I had in mind would be fair," I said.

"Oh? Who's that?"

"Asa Lubbock."

"Lubbock? Is he still around?"

I nodded. "If I could get him, would you agree to take the problem to court?"

"Asa Lubbock," Flexx repeated. "Old Lawbook himself. He's famous throughout the country for sticking to the letter of the law in all his cases."

Finally he looked me straight in the eye. "Like my ancestors, I'm a gambler," he said. "So okay. With Asa Lubbock sitting on the bench, I'll let a court decide whether Horace, Essie, and Ellsworth are people or not."

"Can . . . can you get Judge Lubbock?" Books whispered in my ear.

"I don't know. But I can try. Horace, where's the telephone?"

"That strange instrument that enables one to talk across the miles? There—in the storage closet, where it's out of sight."

Inside the closet I looked up Asa Lubbock's number and punched the buttons on the phone. One ring. Two . . .

"Yes?" said a harsh voice. "What is it?"

"Judge Lubbock?"

"This is he. And to whom am I speaking?"

"Tommy Donahue, sir. And I—"

"I told you, Thomas, there'd be no further interviews. So if you—"

"No, judge! Don't hang up. I have something for you."

"A gift? I don't accept—"

"No, sir. It's . . . well . . . about the ghosts."

"Ghosts?" asked Judge Lubbock in amazement. "Thomas, are you somehow involved with those . . . those apparitions who are said to inhabit Parnell House?"

"Yes, sir."

"You're sure you're not dreaming all this?"

"I'm sure. The ghosts are in the living room right now. They want to know if, according to the law, they're people or not."

"Well, I'm sure I don't know. . . ."

"Neither does anybody else. That's why we need a trial."

"A trial? Is that why you called me?"

"Yes, sir. There's going to be a trial, and we want you to be the judge."

"But I'm retired. I couldn't possibly . . . No, Thomas. The answer is no."

"But there isn't anybody else that both sides will accept. If you don't help us now, we'll never find out what the law really says about ghosts."

"The law!" Judge Lubbock snapped. "The law recognizes every human—"

"I know. But we still don't know if ghosts are included as humans."

The silence on the line seemed to last forever. Then I heard the judge's voice again.

"Then it's time the law made up its mind," he said. "Thomas, I'll sit as judge for this case. When will the trial be?"

"Why . . . uh . . . sometime in the next few days, I

guess. It'd have to be after dark. That's the only time the ghosts can appear."

"Very well. The usual courtroom hours will be altered in view of the ghosts' problem."

"Great!" I was really excited. "And the trial will be right here in Parnell House, and—"

"No, Thomas."

"What do you mean, no? I thought you'd agreed to—"

"If there's to be a trial, it must be held in the Village Hall. I will not hear a case unless it be from a proper bench in a proper courtroom."

"But the ghosts can't leave this house, and—"

"No buts, Thomas. I've already made one ruling in favor of the ghosts. If they want to be considered people, they must be in court at the proper time. About this I remain adamant."

"I tell you we can't—"

"I've made my ruling. You will either abide by it or drop the case. I'll wait here by the telephone exactly thirty minutes for your decision."

I walked morosely out of the closet. "From the look on your face, Tommy," said Ellsworth Parnell, "I assume you were unsuccessful in engaging Asa Lubbock's services."

"I thought it'd be too much for the old geezer,"

boomed Hiram Flexx. "Turned you down flat, did he?"

"He was all set to do it," I replied. "Only . . ."

"Only what?" asked Essie.

"He insisted that we all had to go to the courtroom down at the Village Hall. And you ghosts can't go there."

"Couldn't they hire a lawyer to speak for them?" asked Flexx.

"I will not abide by the judgment of any court," said Essie firmly, "if I can't be there when the case is presented. I might have a few important things to say."

"I feel the same," said Ellsworth. "But once having taken refuge in Parnell House, it seems we ghosts cannot go beyond its walls."

"You're stuck," said Flexx with a grin. "So how about giving some thought to putting on a show for the tourists? At least you'll have something to do while you're—"

"Hold," said Horace, setting his head onto his shoulders. "Hold a bit. Let me think. Ah, yes. Yes indeed."

"What's up, Horace?" I asked.

"'Tis true, Young Thomas, that we ghosts are in a

sense prisoners here in Parnell House. And yet—"

"Get to the point, Horace!" demanded Books.

"There is one night—one magic night a year—when all ghosts may travel to wherever their fancy takes them."

"When, Horace?" Essie cried out excitedly. "When is that night?"

"The eve before All Saints' Day," he answered. "The last night of October. For a few short hours graves give up the ghosts of the dead, and spirits and goblins and beings both wonderful and terrible consort with humans. The festival is celebrated among the living, I understand, with fanciful dress and pranks and parties. Never before now have Essie and I felt the need to leave Parnell House and possibly frighten young children on that night. But now—"

"Halloween!" I shouted. "And it's only two days—I mean nights—away."

"If we can indeed travel to the courtroom, then perhaps, Tommy, you should call Judge Lubbock before he has a change of heart."

I made the call. Asa Lubbock was really excited that he was going to judge one more case—especially one where there'd be ghosts. "What about time, though?" he asked me. "How long will we have before the ghosts have to return to their house?"

I asked Horace.

"We will be transported back here at the stroke of midnight," he told me. I passed word along to the judge.

"The regular business of the court will take until about six o'clock," he said. "We should be ready by seven."

"I'll have Mayor Peace see to it," I said.

"Five hours—not much time for a court case, Thomas. I hope both sides are well represented by counsel. Well, good-bye, young man. I will expect to see all parties to this case on Halloween."

I hung up the phone. "The judge mentioned counsel," I said. My head was spinning. There was so much to do and so little time.

"That means lawyers, doesn't it?"

"Not necessarily," rumbled Flexx. "I don't think I'll have any trouble proving ghosts aren't people. I intend to handle my own case."

"How about you ghosts?" I asked. "You'll need somebody. Maybe my father—"

"No, Thomas," said Essie. She and Horace and Ellsworth were all shaking their heads back and forth.

"Then who? . . ."

"You, Young Thomas, and Books and Harry," said Horace, "have always been our knights and protectors whenever Parnell House was endangered. Why then should we not depend on the three of you once more?"

"You want *us* to represent you?" asked Harry the Blimp in astonishment.

"We do. Whatever be the outcome, we'll know you did your best."

"I'm going to have three kids working against me," chuckled Hiram Flexx. "In front of Old Lawbook. Hey, this is going to be easy—a real piece of cake. Haw, haw, haw!"

* * *

When I got home that night, Mom gave me a long lecture about how I was spending too much time with the ghosts and needed to see more real people for a change.

"It's very late," she finished up. "Your father's in his office. Go say good night to him and then off to bed with you. I want you all tucked in with the light off by ten thirty."

When I told Dad about how I'd gotten Hiram Flexx to agree to a trial, he about flipped.

"Tommy, that's . . . well, it's incredible. Ghosts on

trial. Even the Supreme Court never handled a case like this. Son, you . . . you just amaze me."

"And Asa Lubbock is coming out of retirement to be the judge."

Dad shook his head in wonder. "Any lawyer in the world would give his right arm to handle such a case," he said. "And you've got it. My boy—an eighth grader—is going to make legal history."

"There's just one thing, Dad," I said.

"What's that, Tommy?"

"Can you tell me everything I need to know about being a lawyer for the ghosts? Talk fast, because Mom said I have to be in bed in fifteen minutes."

Courtroom

The next morning Dad did something I never thought would happen.

He got Books and Harry the Blimp and me out of school for two whole days. And we weren't even sick.

We all met with Mrs. Cobb in the principal's office, and Dad explained about what was happening at Parnell House and how we three were going to be "lawyers" for the ghosts. When he'd finished, Mrs. Cobb spoke up.

"It seems to me that for the next two days these youngsters would get a lot more education by preparing their case than by attending classes," she told the principal, Mr. Block. "And I'm sure they can make up any work they miss."

Mr. Block didn't seem too sure about that. But he finally agreed to give us the time off.

Back at our house Dad took us into his office and gave us a little pep talk.

"You three were really smart to get this court case set up," he said. "But you see, whether or not the ghosts are people doesn't make any difference."

"How come?" asked Harry the Blimp. "If they *are* people, they can just . . ."

"Just what, Harry?" asked Dad. "No matter who owns Parnell House, the ghosts can't leave—unless Flexx kicks 'em out."

"You've got something up your sleeve, Mr. Donahue," said Books. "Some idea. What is it?"

"Whatever Judge Lubbock decides about Horace, Essie, and Ellsworth, Hiram Flexx will still own Parnell House. Unless . . ."

"Unless what, Dad?"

"Unless—somehow—you can prove that poker game wasn't honest."

"How could we do that, Mr. Donahue?" Books asked. "I mean, that game happened eighty years ago. And both the mayor and Ellsworth Parnell said there was no proof of cheating."

"True," said Dad. "But to me it just doesn't stand to reason that Addison Flexx could win every big pot for three days. He must have had some gimmick. If you could prove the game wasn't on the up-and-up, we could easily . . . Well, it's just something for you to think about while you're preparing for the trial."

"But we don't know anything about poker," said Books.

"You've got two days to find out about both poker and the law. Unless you can prove there was something wrong with that game on the *Titanic*, you can say good-bye to Parnell House."

Dad drove us downtown to the public library. "There's a big law section in the research area," he said as we got out of the car. "Look up ghosts and poker and anything else you think would help. By the way, it might be best for the three of you to work separately. That way, one of you might come up with an idea the others never thought of."

The research librarian tried to be helpful. But when we asked her about law cases with ghosts, she almost laughed in our faces.

"Ghosts? Like the ones in Parnell House? Dear me, no. We have nothing about ghosts in court." Then she turned away and kind of snickered.

By the end of the day, Books had found just one case about a ghost. A woman back in 1899 claimed her father came back two days after his death to change his will. The case was thrown out of court.

Harry the Blimp had made a lot of scribbled notes about laws that had to do with gambling.

I went to the encyclopedia, where I looked up "poker" and "card games" and even *"Titanic."* The articles were kind of interesting, but they didn't tell me a single thing I could use in court. By evening I didn't have even one note.

Same thing the next day—Halloween. Harry went searching among the law books, and when he saw something he wanted, he wrote it down until he had about ten pages of stuff. Books took off among the stacks, and when she returned, she had a wad of photocopies with her.

Me? I knew the poker hand that Wild Bill Hickok held when he was shot, and how to play cribbage, and how much the *Titanic* weighed. But nothing to put in the ol' notebook. I could have returned it to the store for a full refund. Tommy Donahue—a klutz to the end. I was ashamed of myself.

Just before we left the library, the three of us flipped coins to decide the order of speaking in court.

Harry the Blimp would be first.

Then Books.

Finally me—last again.

We all ate supper at our house. We had fish because Mom said we needed some brain food.

About six thirty Dad took us downtown to the courtroom. Mom came too. She said she wouldn't miss seeing this case for the world.

We were the first ones there. Mom and Dad took seats in the back. Harry, Books, and I sat at one of the two tables in front of the high judge's bench.

Hiram Flexx came in. He carried a big leather case stuffed full of papers, and on his face was a kind of smirk.

There was no sign of the three Parnell ghosts.

At exactly five minutes before seven the door behind the bench opened. Ms. O'Casey wheeled Asa Lubbock into the courtroom. He was wearing a black judge's robe.

He got stiffly to his feet, and Ms. O'Casey helped him climb up to his big chair. He looked through some papers until . . .

Bang! At exactly seven o'clock the judge pounded his gavel loudly. "This court is now in session," he announced. "All who have business before it come forward and you shall be heard. Since the regular court stenographer is not available, Ms. O'Casey will keep a record of the proceedings. Are you ready, Ms. O'Casey?"

"Yes, your honor."

"Be sure to get down every word."

"I will, your honor. You know how good my shorthand is."

"I do indeed, Ms. O'Casey. Mr. Flexx, are you prepared to begin?"

"I am, your honor."

"And the three . . . uh . . . attorneys for the ghosts. How about—"

Suddenly Harry stood up. "Hey, we can't start yet, your . . . your wonder."

Loud laughter—not only from Flexx, but from Mom and Dad and the Peaces. Harry the Blimp's face got real red.

Bang!

Again the gavel pounded. "Order in the court!" snapped Judge Lubbock. "We'll have no levity here.

And Mr. Troy, the term is 'your honor'—not 'your wonder.'"

"Yes . . . your honor," mumbled Harry. "But the ghosts aren't here yet. So we can't . . ."

With that, Hiram Flexx got up. "The time of this hearing was seven o'clock," he said. "I am prepared to begin. If my opponents are not, then I ask for a summary judgment in my favor."

"Your point is well taken, Mr. Flexx," said the judge. "So without further ado, I—"

"It's not fair!" Books protested.

"This is my courtroom, young lady," said the judge sternly. "The law requires promptness in all proceedings. Therefore I . . ."

Before he could continue, Horace and Essie and Ellsworth Parnell appeared, faint and transparent, in front of the high bench. They got more and more solid until you couldn't tell them from real people—except that Horace was holding his head under his arm, and Essie was dripping water all over the place.

Bang!

"In the interests of . . . of decorum, all those appearing in this court shall keep their heads on their shoulders," the judge ordered. "I assume there's nothing to be done about the . . . eh . . . dampness."

Horace placed his head on top of his body. Essie curtsied politely. Ellsworth took off his derby.

"Now then," Judge Lubbock went on. "Why are you three late?"

"Never having been out of our house before, we lost our way," replied Horace. "We wouldn't be here yet if a pair of little monsters hadn't pointed us in the proper direction."

"Little monsters?" said the judge with a trace of a smile. "That's hardly the way one should refer to the children of our village."

"But they *were* little monsters," said Essie. "One was wearing a witch's mask, with warts and green skin. The other had bandages wrapped about him like an Egyptian mummy."

"Ah, yes. Halloween. I'd forgotten," said Judge Lubbock.

He nodded to Ms. O'Casey, who began jotting down shorthand.

"The question before this court," the judge continued, "is whether ghosts are indeed people, entitled to the protection of the law, or whether they are chattel—mere property—with which the owner of their home can do as he likes."

I remembered what Dad had told us. The *real*

question, I said to myself, is what happened in that poker game.

"Before going any further," Asa Lubbock went on, "I want both sides in this case to understand that we have here a most unusual situation. Because of the . . . uh . . . ghosts, this court can sit only until midnight. Furthermore, there can be no appeal to a higher court. Whatever is decided here must be accepted by all those concerned."

Judge Lubbock peered down at the table where we were seated.

"Briefly, what I say goes," he went on. "Is that clear to everyone?"

"Yes, your honor," said Flexx. Books and Harry and I nodded.

"Attorneys for the ghosts must speak up," said the judge, "so that Ms. O'Casey can record their answer."

"Yes, your honor," we all said together.

"Very well. Mr. Flexx, I'll hear your side first."

Flexx got to his feet and waddled toward the bench. "My case is very simple," he rumbled. "I recently came into an inheritance. It was a deed to Parnell House, originally obtained by my great-grandfather Addison Flexx from Ellsworth Parnell, the ghost over there. He and the other ghosts now reside in the house. I have no objection to their moving out, but since they can't, and since I now own the place, I say that—"

Books got up and raised a hand high over her head. "Your honor, I object!"

"State the nature of your objection, young lady."

"Flexx said just this past Monday that Mayor Peace had ten days to sign over the property. So Parnell House still belongs to the village, doesn't it?"

"Technically, I suppose you're right, Miss Scofield," said Judge Lubbock. "But because of the unusual nature of this hearing, I'm inclined to—"

"But we've still got time to prove it doesn't belong to him."

"Hmm. A rather odd point. Still, I would ask you, Mr. Flexx, to establish your claim to the Parnell estate."

"Of course, your honor," replied Flexx in a bored voice. "It shouldn't take more than a few minutes. You see, I have a deed to—"

Books sprang to her feet. "I object!"

"And just what is your objection now?" the judge asked her.

"We've already seen the deed. But why don't you

ask him how he got it?"

"Miss Scofield, it is your job to ask the questions. I have no intention of—"

"Your honor," said Flexx. "In view of the youth of my worthy opponents, I see no harm in indulging their little whims. I'd be happy to show how I came into possession of the deed. If I may call my first witness . . ."

"Certainly, Mr. Flexx."

"I'd like that ghost—Ellsworth Parnell—to take the stand."

Ellsworth came forward. Ms. O'Casey took a small Bible from her purse. "Do you swear to tell the truth, the whole truth, and nothing but . . ." As she gave the oath, Ellsworth tried his best to keep a hand on the Bible without slipping through it.

"I do," he said.

"Mr. Parnell," said Flexx, "in the interests of saving time, would you tell us in your own words about how you lost the deed to my great-grandfather in a poker game?"

Ellsworth repeated the story of his sailing on the *Titanic* and of the three men he'd played cards with. Finally he got to that last hand.

"I had the seven through jack of hearts—a

nearly unbeatable hand. So I bet heavily. Charles Minton was already out of the game, and soon Lyle Arbuthnot tossed in his three tens. Addison seemed quite upset that Lyle would expose his cards in that manner. However, Flexx and I agreed to play out the hand.

"I'd raise, and Addison would raise back. Soon I had nothing left except the deed with which to bet. I lost to Addison's royal flush."

"An honest reply," said Flexx. He reached into his case and pulled out a piece of paper yellow with age.

"I have here, sir, the original deed to Parnell House. My lawyer sent it to me especially for this hearing. I ask you to examine it."

He held it up for Ellsworth's inspection. "On the back here—is that your signature, assigning the property to my great-grandfather?"

"It is," said Ellsworth mournfully.

"Then I have no more questions. But I offer this deed as evidence of my ownership of Parnell House."

The judge nodded and took the deed. Then he looked over at our table. "Do any of you wish to cross-examine the witness?"

The three of us shook our heads glumly. There wasn't a question we could think of that would help.

"The witness is excused," said Judge Lubbock. "Go on, Mr. Flexx."

"I have little more, your honor. I regret that, while my great-grandfather escaped the *Titantic* tragedy, Ellsworth Parnell went down with the ship. However, I believe I've proved that the house is—or shortly will be—mine. I hold that the ghosts, being officially dead, are no longer human. They are, like the furniture or other items, mere property, which I can keep or dispose of as I wish. That, briefly, is my case."

Judge Lubbock stared at the ceiling for a long time. "Up to a point," he said finally, "the court is inclined to agree with you, Mr. Flexx. If we apply our laws to ghosts, it might make a mockery of the rights of the living. So *if*—and I say *if*—you own the house, your rights are paramount. You can make any arrangement about the ghosts that you care to."

Bang! He pounded his gavel loudly.

Harry and I looked at each other with worried expressions. If the judge was going to rule for Hiram Flexx about everything, then we were . . .

"Hey!" Books shouted. "Don't we get a chance?"

"All sides will be heard, fairly and justly," said Asa Lubbock. "But be warned, Books, Thomas, and Harry, that I am reluctant to consider ghosts as being 'human' under the law. I would advise you to stick to arguments concerning the legal ownership of Parnell House."

Okay. That was what we really wanted to talk about.

I just wished I had something to say.

"Which one of you will be speaking against Mr. Flexx's position?" the judge asked.

"All of us," said Harry. "One at a time."

"I see. Well, as long as you realize we have only until midnight. Who will begin?"

"I will." Harry the Blimp got up and looked at his notes from the library. "Did you know, Judge, that gambling is illegal in this state?"

"I'm aware of it, Mr. Troy."

"And if the police find any money that's been bet, they can take it?"

"I'm quite familiar with the law," said the judge. "In my time I've fined and even jailed gamblers from this very bench."

From the corner of my eye, I saw Essie turn to Ellsworth and Horace. "How clever of Harry to make that point," she said. "If the judge has punished other gamblers, how can Mr. Flexx possibly—"

"Just what are you getting at, Mr. Troy?" asked Judge Lubbock.

"Mr. Flexx admits that his great-grandfather got the deed by gambling. And since the deed is now in this state, where you're not supposed to gamble, I say that—"

Bang!

The judge's angry stare seemed to bore holes right through Harry. "Your reasoning is outrageous, even for a youth!" Lubbock snapped. "I remind you, young man, that the gambling in question took place not here, but on a ship at sea. Furthermore, the *Titanic* sank in 1912—years before our state law was written."

"But . . . "

"Sit down, sir. While I applaud your zeal to protect your friends the ghosts, I reject your reasoning as a matter of law. So if you have nothing more to say, let us continue with someone else."

"Oh, poor Harry!" moaned Essie.

"And poor us," added Horace.

Books and I looked at one another warily. "Harry sure got told off," I whispered.

"Yeah," she said. "Old Lubbock is one tough judge."

"Your turn, Books. Try not to get him any madder than he is already."

Books got up. "Judge," she said, holding a paper in her hand. "I've got some stuff here about the odds against different hands in the game of poker. D'you promise not to get sore if I read 'em?"

"Read away, Miss Scofield. I'll try to keep my temper in check."

"According to Ellsworth Parnell, Addison Flexx held a royal flush," said Books, glancing at the paper. "The odds against that are 649,739 to 1. In the same hand, Ellsworth Parnell had five cards in a row, all in hearts—a straight flush. The odds against that are 72,192 to 1.

"Now to figure the odds of two hands like that getting drawn in the same game, you multiply those two big numbers together. And what would you get?

"The odds would be nearly fifty *billion* against it happening," she announced. "Why, if you played for twenty lifetimes, you might never see anything like that. Come on, your honor. You know there was something fishy about that hand. Addison Flexx must have—"

"Cheated!" I heard Horace whisper. "Well done indeed, Books. Now you have Mr. Flexx on the run. The judge will have to rule . . ."

Hiram Flexx rose from his chair. "If it please the court," he said, "I do hate to interrupt this interesting argument. But according to my great-grandfather's diary, Charles Minton—*not* Addison Flexx—was dealing the hand in question. So how could my great-grandfather have—"

"I don't know!" Books said loudly. "Maybe Flexx and Minton planned this together. Ellsworth Parnell gets a good hand so he'll bet a lot. But Addison Flexx has a better one so he'll win. What do you think of that, your honor?"

Smiling happily, the three ghosts began whispering together. "We're winning," I heard Ellsworth whisper.

Asa Lubbock tapped the bench gently with his gavel.

"Outside this courtroom, Miss Scofield," he said, "I might find your argument quite persuasive. The likelihood of these circumstances does seem remote."

"You bet it does!" replied Books. "So I claim that Addison Flexx and Charles Minton cheated

Ellsworth Parnell out of that deed. To keep things honest, the deed ought to be given back."

"Your point about the deed's being returned if there were cheating is well taken," said the judge. "I'm sure Mr. Flexx would agree."

"We'd *all* agree," said Essie, earning a scowl from the judge.

"Of course I'd agree," said Flexx. "*If* there were cheating. However . . . well, I'm sure your honor would like to make his own ruling."

"While such a set of hands in an honest game is unlikely," Asa Lubbock went on, "it is possible. And in our country, a man is presumed innocent until proved guilty. Proof—that's what's lacking in your argument, Miss Scofield. Definite proof of cheating. So . . ."

"Oh, no!" Essie cried out. The judge droned on, but all his words said the same thing. He wasn't buying Books's argument. I was the only one left who could help the ghosts.

I flipped the pages of my notebook, where I was expected to have all kinds of great things to say. But the pages—every one of 'em—were blank. And in a minute or two I was supposed to get up and start talking.

About what?

I stared down at my hands, flat on the tabletop. Panic started flipping my stomach around like a volleyball. Just to calm myself down I counted the fingers on my left hand:

One—two—three—four—five.

Then the right:

Six—seven—eight—nine—ten.

Up there on the bench, Lubbock was coming to the end of his lecture. In a few minutes everybody in the room would know what a jerk I was.

One—two—three—four—five.

"Therefore, Miss Scofield, I must reject your arguments before this court, clever as they were. And so . . ."

Six—seven—eight—nine—ten.

" . . . we come to the third and last of our young advocates."

One—two—three—four—five.

"Thomas Donahue, it's your turn."

Six—sev . . .

Suddenly, there it was—inside my head.

The answer. The poker game *hadn't* been fair. And I knew why.

I stood up. It was past nine o'clock on Halloween night.

But for me the sun was shining and the birds were singing and everything in the whole world was beautiful.

Because Hiram Flexx would never own Parnell House. It would belong to the ghosts forever.

The End of the Case

For a moment I just stood there, looking around the courtroom—from the judge and Ms. O'Casey up in front, to Mom, Dad, and Alonzo and Cora Peace sitting in back. I knew what I wanted to do, but I had to figure out how.

"Your honor?" I said finally.

"Yes, Thomas?"

"Can . . . can I call on people and ask 'em questions? Just like lawyers do?"

"Of course," said the judge. "However, I do hope you have a better case to make than your two friends did."

"I think so, sir. The first person . . . uh . . . ghost I'd like to talk to is Ellsworth Parnell."

"I object!" bawled Hiram Flexx. "Mr. Parnell has already been questioned by me about that last hand of cards. These kids had a chance to ask questions then."

"But I don't want to know about that last hand," I replied. "I want to ask him something else."

"We're here to get all the facts," the judge ruled. "So you may question the . . . the ghost, Thomas. When you ask your questions, I'll decide if they're proper or not."

He pointed toward Ellsworth with his gavel. "Mr. Parnell, take the stand. I remind you, you're still under oath to tell the truth."

Ellsworth walked—actually, he kind of drifted—to the witness stand. "Mr. Parnell . . ." I began.

"Call me Ellsworth," said the ghost. "We're friends, aren't we, Tommy?"

"Yes, sir—I mean Ellsworth. Will you tell us about the cards that were used in the game? Where did you get them?"

"But Tommy, I already spoke of that when we were back in—"

Bang! Judge Lubbock pounded his gavel like he was driving fence posts. "I have no way of knowing about conversations made outside this courtroom," he told Ellsworth. "Just answer the question."

"The cards were provided by a ship's steward. Two decks, both sealed in boxes."

"What did they look like?"

"They were blue. They said *'Titanic'* on the back."

"Both decks were the same?"

"Yes."

"Then if they got mixed together, I guess there'd be no way of telling which cards belonged in which deck. Is that right?"

"Well . . . I suppose so, now that you—"

Bang!

"If you're suggesting there might have been some trickery with the cards," snapped Judge Lubbock, "then your question is out of order, young man. I've already ruled that any question of cheating has to be proved beyond a reasonable doubt."

"I didn't say anything about cheating, sir." Not *yet,* I added to myself. "I just wanted everybody to know what the cards looked like."

"Now we know," said the judge sternly. "I'd suggest you go on to some other subject, Thomas."

"Okay," I said. "That's all I wanted to ask you,

Ellsworth. Thanks a lot."

"The witness may step down." Asa Lubbock leaned across the high bench and glared at me. "If that's all you have to add to these proceedings, then—"

"No, your honor. I want to talk to somebody else."

"Who?"

"Mayor Peace."

"What?" Alonzo, sitting in the back of the courtroom, was puzzled. "Why me? I wasn't on the *Titanic* during those poker games. I wasn't even born yet. So I can't tell you anything about—"

"I must object!" added Flexx. "Mr. Peace wants to keep me from owning Parnell House. So anything he says about those games on the *Titanic* would be unfair and prejudiced."

The judge tapped his gavel. "Attorneys for both sides will approach the bench."

Flexx got up and walked forward. I was a little confused until Judge Lubbock beckoned for me to come up too.

"Mr. Flexx has a point," the judge told me as I stood looking up at him. "You can't ask the mayor about how those four men were playing."

"But I don't want to ask him about that," I said.

"Then what . . ."

"I just want to ask him about . . . about the rules of poker. How it's played. That kind of stuff."

"Ah, I see. An expert witness on the subject of poker. But I warn you, Thomas—not one question or even one word about the *Titanic* games. Do you understand me?"

"Yes."

"Then your objection is overruled, Mr. Flexx. Let's get on with the case."

Judge Lubbock looked out at the mayor. "Alonzo Peace is called to the stand as an expert on the game of poker!" he ordered loudly.

"Poker!" Suddenly Cora Peace, Alonzo's wife, was on her feet. "What do you mean, an expert?"

Bang! "You're out of order, Mrs. Peace."

"I don't care. Alonzo never told me he played poker."

She glared down at her husband, whose face was bright red.

"You told me all those times you went out in the evening that you had special meetings of the Village Council!" she screeched. "You never said anything about poker, Alonzo Peace!"

"Now, Cora," he mumbled. "Don't get so upset.

We just had a few pleasant little games after the meetings ended."

"A few games? Sometimes you didn't get home until after midnight! Oh, you just wait until I get you home! I'll soon put an end to this poker business!"

Bang! "This courtroom is no place to settle personal problems," said the judge. "Though I must say, mayor, I'd hate to be in your shoes right now. However, I must order you to come forward and testify."

Cora Peace glared at Alonzo as he got up and walked to the witness stand.

"Remember, Thomas," said Judge Lubbock. "Just the rules, and how the game is played. Not one single word about—"

"Yes, sir."

Alonzo took the oath from Ms. O'Casey and sat down uneasily in the witness chair. From the look on his face, he was awful angry with me.

"Will you tell us about the deck of cards used in a poker game?" I asked.

"There are fifty-two cards," the mayor muttered between clenched teeth. "The four suits are hearts, diamonds, clubs, and spades. What else do you want to know?"

"How many cards of each kind are in a deck?"

"Why, four. Everybody knows that. Four aces, four twos, four threes . . . Come on, Tommy. They're the same cards you youngsters play rummy with."

"Okay. Now on the *Titanic* Ellsworth Parnell had a straight—"

Bang! "No, Thomas. You can't ask about the *Titanic.*"

"Yeah, I understand. I just made a mistake. Mayor, in poker, what's a jack-high straight flush?"

From the corner of my eye, I saw Ellsworth whispering to Horace and Essie.

"It would be the seven, eight, nine, ten, jack—all in the same suit."

I spread my hands and counted the fingers again.

One—two—three—four—five . . .

Six—seven—eight—nine—ten.

"How about a royal flush?"

"It's nothing more than an ace-high straight flush. Ten, jack, queen, king, ace—again, all in the same suit."

"Thanks, Mayor. That's all I wanted to know, so I guess you can go back and sit down. And I'm real sorry I got you in trouble with Mrs. Peace."

"Thomas," said Judge Lubbock, "you seem to be

getting at something here. But I must say I don't understand what. Do you intend to call any more witnesses?"

"No. I mean . . . well . . ."

"I'm aware you're not a real lawyer. So if you're confused, perhaps I can help you."

"Then tell me, your honor—does Ms. O'Casey have everything we've said written down? I mean, every *word*?"

"Every word," said the judge. "Her shorthand is absolutely perfect. But why do you ask?"

"Is it all right if I ask her about something that happened earlier?"

"Testimony can always be repeated. Ms. O'Casey, will you help Thomas?"

Ms. O'Casey put down her pencil and looked over at me.

"I want to go back to the first time Ellsworth was on the stand," I said. "When Mr. Flexx was asking him questions."

Ms. O'Casey shuffled through her papers.

"He was talking about the cards he had."

"Here it is," she said. "'I had the seven through . . .'"

"A little further," I told her. "Something about Lyle Arbuthnot."

"'Lyle Arbuthnot tossed in his three tens. Addison seemed . . .' "

All of a sudden just about everybody in the courtroom was laughing and shouting and chattering to one another. Horace and Essie and Ellsworth had big smiles on their faces and were disappearing and then appearing again in excitement. In the back Mayor Peace had forgotten about his troubles with his wife and was slapping my father on the back. Books and Harry the Blimp were pounding their table in glee. Even Judge Lubbock was leaning back in his chair and chuckling loudly.

Hiram Flexx, however, wasn't too happy.

"I object, your honor!" he howled

"On what grounds, Mr. Flexx?" asked the judge.

"Why . . . why, on the grounds that the ghost of Ellsworth Parnell might have been lying when—"

"No, Mr. Flexx. Your objection is overruled. It is the opinion of this court that Ellsworth Parnell told the absolute truth, even when it hurt his case to do so."

"But—"

"Furthermore, the ghost was your own witness. And right after he'd made that remark about Lyle Arbuthnot's cards, you said . . . Would you read Mr.

Flexx's remark, Ms. O'Casey?"

Her finger still marked the place in her notes. "He said that the ghost—Ellsworth Parnell—made 'An honest reply.' Those were Flexx's exact words."

"'An honest reply' one time, and 'lying' later?" said the judge. "You can't have it both ways, Hiram Flexx. Now sit down!"

Judge Lubbock turned back to me. "You have a good case, Thomas," he said. "And you've handled it well. But for the court records I'll have to ask you to tell what all this testimony means, so Ms. O'Casey can write it down."

"It's simple," I replied, looking down at my fingers. "Ellsworth Parnell's cards included a ten. Addison Flexx had another ten in his hand. Then Lyle Arbuthnot laid down three more tens. That's five tens."

I looked over to where Hiram Flexx sat, his face as gloomy as a thundercloud.

"But there are only four tens in any deck of cards," I went on. "Something was wrong in that game!"

"I will not sit here and have my great-grandfather accused of cheating," roared Flexx.

"Nobody," said the judge, "has accused anyone of

anything, Mr. Flexx. Perhaps the extra ten got into play by accident. After all, there was another deck of cards there with the same design. The only fact this court will rule on is that there were indeed five tens in play during the hand in which Ellsworth Parnell lost the deed to his house. That being the case, the hands and the betting and everything else were not legitimate. It was, in poker terms, a misdeal. Therefore the transfer of deed to Addison Flexx and his descendants is declared null and void."

I turned to Books. "What does that mean?" I asked.

"It means Flexx loses," she said. I saw her eyes fill with tears of joy. "You did it, Tommy! Parnell House still belongs to Bramton . . . and the ghosts."

Bang!

"Hiram Flexx, I am turning the deed over to Mayor Peace at once," announced Judge Lubbock.

Bang! "This court is adjourned!"

Suddenly the three ghosts were all gathered about me. "Well done, Young Thomas!" said Horace. He tried to pat me on the back. His hand went right through me. I felt a shiver go up my spine.

"Oh, Tommy, we're all jus' so proud!" exclaimed Essie.

"You saved me from the consequences of my folly in playing cards for such high stakes," said Ellsworth. "I am forever in your debt, young fellow."

Suddenly Horace looked at the clock in the courtroom. "It's well over an hour before midnight comes," he said. "Still All Hallow's Eve. I wonder . . ."

"Wonder what?" Essie asked him.

"Trick or treat," Horace replied. "The children seemed to have such fun with it. Do you suppose we three ghosts could—"

"Don't you even think of such a thing, Horace Parnell!" Essie said firmly. "Why, if we were to appear at people's houses with me dripping water and you holding your head in your arms and Ellsworth all white with those blue lips, the citizens of Bramton would purely die of fright."

"But I'd like some candy!" pouted Horace.

"Oh, pooh, you ol' devil. You haven't eaten a thing in over two hundred years. Now let's return to Parnell House, where we belong. Harry, Books, Tommy—you come along too. We'll have a party of our own. It'll be the best Halloween party in the whole world—because it'll have *real* ghosts."

* * *

That's about all there is to tell. Hiram Flexx left

Bramton the next day, and none of us ever heard from him again. It cost Alonzo Peace a brand-new winter coat and a pearl necklace to get back on the good side of his wife.

As for me, the trial gave me plenty of stuff to write in my essay about Asa Lubbock. The mark I got from Mrs. Cobb was an A+.

Books and Harry the Blimp and I still visit Parnell House one or two evenings a week. We walk down Spring Street, to where the old place stands on its three acres of land with the family graveyard out in back. We go inside and turn on the lights, and the ghosts appear, and we have all kinds of fun. The ghosts tell spooky stories, or we make up riddles, or sometimes we play draughts—checkers—on the old board in the bedroom.

But we never . . . *never* . . . play cards.

About the Author

BILL BRITTAIN's tales of the rural New England village of Coven Tree are well loved by children of all ages. THE WISH GIVER was a 1984 Newbery Honor Book; it and DEVIL'S DONKEY were both named ALA Notable Children's Books as well as School Library Journal Best Books. The third Coven Tree novel, DR. DREDD'S WAGON OF WONDERS, was a 1988 Children's Editors' Choice (ALA Booklist), and the fourth, PROFESSOR POPKIN'S PRODIGIOUS POLISH, was named a "Pick of the Lists" by American Bookseller.

Mr. Brittain has written many other delightful books, including ALL THE MONEY IN THE WORLD, which won the 1982–1983 Charlie May Simon Children's Book Award and was adapted for television as an ABC–TV Saturday Special. His fast-paced mystery WHO KNEW THERE'D BE GHOSTS?, a companion to THE GHOST FROM BENEATH THE SEA, was a Children's

Choice for 1986 (IRA/CBC), and THE FANTASTIC FRESHMAN was named a Children's Choice for 1989 and an ALA Recommended Book for Reluctant Young Adult Readers. The comedy-thriller MY BUDDY, THE KING was a Children's Choice for 1990.

The author of over 65 mystery stories, which have appeared in *Ellery Queen's Mystery Magazine*, *Alfred Hitchcock's Mystery Magazine*, and several anthologies, Bill Brittain lives with his wife, Ginny, in Asheville, North Carolina.

About the Artist

MICHELE CHESSARE is a graduate of the Rhode Island School of Design. She has illustrated Bill Brittain's WHO KNEW THERE'D BE GHOSTS? as well as *The Horn Book*'s 1988 Fanfare Honor List book ROOMRIMES, by Sylvia Cassedy.

Ms. Chessare lives in Peachtree City, Georgia.